so weird

Escape

Created by Tom J. Astle

Adapted by Elizabeth M. Rees

Based on the television script
by Doug Jung

Disney
PRESS

New York

Prologue

What would it feel like to spread my arms and fly right out of my body right now? Would I be able to float over mountains? Would I be able to get back?

Have you ever thought about leaving your body? Like during a math test, when you forgot to study, or maybe just because it would be cool to spread your arms and go flying?

Well, for thousands of years there have been people who believed they could do exactly that. They say that a person's spirit can actually leave its sleeping body and travel around by itself.

What blows me away is that so many cultures, all over the world, throughout history, believe in some sort of astral projection.

Some people say they can get out of their bodies by ritual dancing, or meditating, or even by getting conked on the head. That wouldn't be my favorite way.

And then there are the ones who say they can do it whenever they want. . . .

Chapter One

Fourteen-year-old Fiona "Fi" Phillips lifted one of the wooden slats on the blind covering the window of the custom tour bus and found herself face-to-face with a huge full moon—tinged an eerie red. The big ball of light hung so low over the Wyoming high country, Fi felt that if she reached out the window she could actually touch it.

Fi, whose name was pronounced "Fee," propped her chin on her hands and watched the moonlit landscape whoosh by. Except for the taillights of her mother Molly's band's crew bus just up ahead, the road was deserted. Even with elk grazing on the frosty stubble, the prairie looked so abandoned, so otherworldly. In the distance, Fi could barely make out the dark, jagged shapes of the Rocky Mountains. They seemed as far off as forever.

It certainly felt like forever since she'd seen a road sign. How far was it to Bardo, anyway? Fi sighed as the bus downshifted and began the gradual climb into the foothills of the Rockies.

Fi imagined what it would be like to fly over those mountains, and giggled softly.

You are sometimes so weird, just like your big bro, Jack, says! Fi had to admit that to imagine flying over the Rockies was a pretty far-out idea. But leaving her body wasn't. A person could really do that. Fi had just found that out tonight, surfing the Web. She'd downloaded a pile of real-life accounts of astral projection.

Jack was just one year older, but she could imagine his reaction if he discovered her latest venture in the world of the mysterious. He'd tell her she was off the deep end again, or at least call her a geek.

Oh, well, let him laugh, Fi thought now, and brushed her bangs out of her eyes.

Fi lowered the slats of the blind and settled back down on her desk chair. Schoolbooks were stacked next to her open laptop on the small desk.

Her closet-sized bedroom was the first of four lined up along one side of the bus. Jack shared the next room with his old pal, Clu. Fi's mom's room was next in line. The last room at the back of the bus was for Irene and Ned Bell—Clu's mom and dad—who worked for Molly on the tour. A narrow corridor running alongside the rooms led to the common area up front behind the driver. Outfitted like a camper, the bus boasted a shower, a bathroom, even a tiny kitchenette. Everything was small and built-in, but very comfortable.

For the most part Fi loved life on the road with her mom's new band. Living on a bus was cramped but fun. Every day brought new adventures as the small troupe crisscrossed the country on Molly Phillips's comeback tour.

Fi folded her legs under her and twirled one of the ears of her bunny slippers as she checked out her computer screen. The file downloading counter was still ticking—two minutes more to go before that intriguing patch she'd found on the "Afterlife" Web site finished downloading.

Except for the dim golden glow of a Lava lamp bubbling on a corner of her desk, and the blue light of the aquarium, Fi's room was dark. She could hear her mom on the other side of the thin partition in the common area, strumming her old acoustic Gibson, shaping the lyrics for a new song.

It was past Fi's bedtime, but Fi was too pumped for sleep. "Download completed!" the pleasant female computer voice she had programmed into her machine announced.

"Thank you," she told her laptop. Wrapping a strand of her long brown hair around her fingers,

Fi thought a moment. She stared unseeing at the bulletin board collaged with clippings, postcards, photos, ticket stubs, and various souvenirs of places they had visited over the past few months.

But then her brown eyes focused on the framed photo of her dad and herself on the bookshelf. She smiled wistfully at the photo of a handsome dark-haired man holding a baby—her. Just a few years later, her dad had been killed in a car accident by a drunk driver. His death had sent the whole family into a tailspin. Mom had quit performing, unable to face being onstage without her husband backing her. Molly had managed to support the family by writing commercial jingles—until now. She had finally decided to re-form her group.

Dad would be happy about this comeback tour, Fi thought, sure of it, just as she was sure he would have hated that her mom's grief had forced her to give up her singing career.

Fi's actual memories of her dad were so vague: the clean soapy scent of his skin, the feel of his soft suede fringed jacket—a jacket Molly still kept in the closet and every so often wore. Even though she had never really known her dad, Fi felt connected to him, as if he somehow was always with her, every day of her life.

Half the time she expected to turn around and catch him standing behind her, smiling as he was in that picture, encouraging her—or when things got scary or she felt terribly alone, protecting her.

Sometimes she thought her interest in the occult, in the mysterious, in everything that had no real explanation in the concrete material world of her everyday life, had to do with her dad's death. She often felt his spirit was still with her. Like tonight. It was the idea that someone could continue to exist outside his body that she found so exciting.

Fi pasted a soft image of rows of meditating figures across the bottom of her Fi's "So Weird" Web page. She'd first designed her site about a year ago, just to kill time on the road.

Before Fi knew it, her page had developed a life of its own, and connected her to some amazing people and sites. Lots of kids on-line shared her passion for anything remotely mysterious.

Not that she'd been on the prowl for mysteries when she had finished her math homework tonight and treated herself to some primo surf-time. She'd been checking out the locale of her mom's next gig: Bardo, Wyoming. They'd arrive tomorrow in the small western town, and Fi loved finding out obscure details about every place the band visited.

So Fi had typed in keyword *Bardo*. But instead of pictures of mountains, rodeos, cowboys, or even just farmland, she hit on a site devoted to Tibet and the afterlife.

Bardo wasn't only the name of a town in the foothills of the Rockies. It was also a place—more like a nonplace—between this life and the next, an in-between realm between the living and the dead. Thinking about that now sent a chill up Fi's spine.

Maybe I forgot to type in the word *Wyoming*, she told herself, trying to shake off a premonition that strange events awaited her arrival in Bardo.

Fi had surfed tonight through at least a dozen hyperlinks, landing finally at a far-out site devoted to astral projection. She had downloaded some amazing images of remote Tibetan monasteries, Egyptian papyri, places in ancient Greece, and then amazing bits of Indian art.

Fi put up some more images on her site. Then she invited any visitors to the site to add their own comments on her bulletin board and to upload more art.

She inserted the small file of audio and video clips, played it back, and watched as figures of tribesmen danced feverishly by firelight. The graceful line of dancers segued smoothly into rows of peacefully meditating Tibetan monks. Pausing to stretch her arms above her head, Fi viewed the screen. "That's a two thumbs up," she congratulated herself. With a click of her mouse, she dragged the image more to one side of the page and changed the shape.

Finally she dragged and pasted her favorite piece of art, a diagram of a sleeping figure with its "astral twin" hovering over it. Looking at the picture made Fi tingle all over.

Fi signed off her computer and crawled into bed. As she drifted off to sleep, she couldn't help but wonder exactly what drifting out of her own body would feel like.

Chapter Two

The big blue-and-silver tour bus was parked outside the Bardo Hotel. Bardo was not at all up to her expectations. Nothing otherworldly or remotely mysterious about this small Wyoming town, Fi thought, disappointed.

She, Jack, and Clu Bell were outside, sitting in one of the open cargo bays of the bus, having an English literature lesson. The band's roadies were bustling back and forth between the buses, the equipment truck, and the Bardo Hotel, unloading baggage and gear for that night's performance at the Bardo Badlands, the hotel's small dance club.

"So, guys, since it's a great autumn day, let's celebrate by reading one of the coolest poems ever written about the season," Ned Bell announced.

"Yuck!" exclaimed Jack. He tugged at his thick short hair. Jack strongly resembled their father, with dark hair and a lopsided, dimpled smile. Except he wasn't smiling now. "Poetry's the pits."

"Like, Dad, do we *have* to?" Clu grumbled, shielding his blue eyes from the sun.

Ned ignored him, opened a small book of

poems, and began to read aloud. Jack propped his back against the wall of the cargo bay. Clu pillowed his head on his arms and closed his eyes.

Fi tried to look like she was paying attention. She liked the *sound* of poems; they reminded her of great song lyrics. But some of this old English stuff lost her.

Ned was determined to turn them all on to poetry. He didn't look like Fi's idea of the poetry type. Ned was a beefy guy with unruly red-blond hair who spoke with a drawl. He looked like a roadie—exactly what he was. Besides driving Molly Phillips's bus, Ned was in charge of the rest of the band and the crew. But beneath his slow easy exterior Ned possessed what Jack called a capital-B Brain. Which is why he was home schooling the kids during the tour. Home schooling was one part of life on the road that Fi hadn't decided if she liked.

Fi stifled a yawn. Maybe surfing the Web half the night wasn't worth it.

A warm October sun bathed the streets of Bardo. At midnight, and miles away, Fi could imagine Bardo as something—well—*different* than this. By day Bardo looked like Anytown, USA.

Fi would die before admitting it to his face, but

this morning she was beginning to think Jack was right: if a person couldn't taste, or smell, or touch something, it didn't exist. Bardo, the afterlife, and out-of-body experiences seemed totally silly by the light of day.

Earlier that afternoon when the tour bus had left the interstate and rolled down Main Street, Fi decided she might as well be back on Main Street in her hometown of Hope Springs, Colorado. The Bardo Hotel was on Aspen Boulevard, and right around the corner lay Cottonwood Lane. Neat rows of white-trimmed brick houses, most of them 1950s vintage, flanked this end of the block. Scarecrows and tall sheaves of corn stalks decorated manicured lawns. Orange pumpkins were perched on porch steps; bundles of colorful Indian corn were tacked on front doors. Heaps of golden leaves were piled near garbage cans waiting for pickup. Everything looked exactly like home.

Exactly like home . . . Fi wondered . . . Wouldn't any normal fourteen-year-old be homesick for her friends and hometown? But Fi honestly wasn't. Her Hope Springs crowd was constantly in touch by E-mail. Fi was sort of a celebrity among her hometown pals, updating them on life on the road and all of her adventures.

Today, however, the only truly *interesting* thing Fi had spotted was a sign advertising a Harvest Carnival Week. The fairgrounds were an easy walk from the Bardo Hotel. But even if she went to the carnival, riding a roller coaster or a Tilt-A-Whirl didn't qualify as an adventure.

Fi toyed with the frayed hem of her old red jeans, then caught Ned frowning at her over the top of the poetry book. Fi straightened her back and tried to look perky and alert.

"So, kids, that about wraps it up for English lit—for today!" Ned's announcement brought Fi right back to the present. Ned stopped pacing and looked at Fi.

Fi shaded her eyes and grinned up at Ned. With any luck he'd end classes early today—if only because they had arrived late and everything was behind schedule.

Fi's grin faded when Ned put the book down on top of one of the chrome-trimmed black trunks that held the band's sound equipment and stood in for desks, then picked up a sheaf of papers.

Ned displayed the papers. "Time to check out these math tests."

"No way!" Clu groaned, and ducked deeper into the cargo bay. Jack rolled his eyes at Clu.

Unlike Jack, Clu hated school; he never read. Having his dad as a teacher was really tough on him—schoolwork was definitely Clu's last priority. Web surfing, skateboards, video games, jamming with Jack on their electric guitars, and lately, girls, were more his speed.

Fi smiled weakly. Though she loved science, her worst subject was math.

"Things in the math department are looking up," Ned announced, surprising Fi.

Clu stopped cringing, and slid back out of the depths of the cargo bay. He dusted off his jeans and smoothed the front of his paisley-print shirt. "Awesome," he said.

Ned avoided Clu's eyes, but beamed at Jack.

Jack beamed back. A+ again, Fi figured, envying her brother's knack for math.

Even before Ned handed Jack his test paper, Jack looked impossibly smug.

"Hundred percent, Jack," Ned congratulated. "Good job."

No surprise there! Fi thought, then crossed her fingers and prayed to the goddess of grades. Please. Just this once. Let me get a B.

"Fi, not bad. Shows you hard work pays off."

Fi's eyes widened as she saw a big, bold B+

penciled in red at the top of her paper. "Gee, thanks!" she exclaimed, delighted.

As Ned turned toward Clu, Jack murmured to Fi, "See what a little brotherly tutoring can do? Do I hear a thank-you?"

"I'm the one who took the test, not you," Fi countered, then rolled her eyes. As much as they teased each other, Fi really was close to her brother and was glad for his help. "T-H-A-N-K-S," she spelled out. "Poor Clu," she mouthed, looking at Clu.

Jack followed Fi's gaze, and winced. Clu was smiling expectantly at his dad, as if his dad were about to hand him a pizza with the works. Clu shook back his longish blond bangs and reached out for his test paper.

Ned cleared his throat and reluctantly handed it over. Heaving a big sigh, he hunkered down in front of Clu and said glumly, "Well, son, I don't know how to say this but . . . how can I put this without lowering your self-esteem . . . I love you, but you did lousy."

Clu's grin vanished. "I did?" He sounded surprised.

Jack rolled his eyes and exchanged a glance with Fi, then quickly turned toward Ned.

"No offense, Mr. B.," Jack butted in. "Maybe it's not Clu's fault."

"It's not?" Clu repeated.

"Why not?" Ned shook his head. "If by hitting the books harder Fi can bring up her grades to a B-plus, so can Clu."

"Hitting the books—well." Jack paused. "Maybe that doesn't work for everyone. At some point the educational system has to take responsibility for our performance, y'know. Come up with a new approach."

"You mean, if Clu flunks, it's my fault?" Ned's face was getting red.

Fi gulped. Ned almost never lost his temper, but he sure looked about to blow now. Last time he'd gotten mad at the kids, when the three of them had short-sheeted the Bells' bed, she, Jack, and Clu had been punished. Jack and Clu had had to give up their video games; Fi had had to stay off her laptop. It had been a real drag.

Jack plunged on. "Of course it's your fault. You're the teacher."

Clu picked up Jack's argument. "Yeah, you have to reach out to us, Dad. Meet us at our level."

Ned laughed.

"I've been on your level." He stood up and

shrugged. "I don't think I'd want to be fifteen again."

Before Ned could go on, Clu jumped up, his blue eyes twinkling mischievously. "Right, Dad. It's way rotten being fifteen or sixteen. You know all about it—firsthand. So you know better than anyone how we need some fun to balance all the hard work."

"Clu, we're talking about your math test, and I'm not sure you even know what work is, let alone 'hard' work when it comes to homework."

Fi was suddenly inspired. "Yeah, but Mr. B., maybe what Clu's getting at is we need a change. We've been on the road a couple of months now, and maybe we need to shake up our routine, get out of our rut," she said, jamming her hands in the pockets of her jeans. "Like, by this time back home in school we'd have had some kind of break—you know, some kind of field trip."

"Your whole life these days is a field trip," Ned countered.

"Not exactly," Jack broke in. "We have school every day."

"Seven days a week," Clu added solemnly. "That's totally like slave labor!"

"For about two hours a day at the most," Ned

defended, turning as one of the roadies called to him.

"Where's this stuff go?" the guy shouted over the drone of a semi braking at the light on the street behind them.

Ned barked some instructions before facing the kids again.

"Mr. B., I know exactly what Clu needs. . . ." Jack pressed on.

"You do?" Clu asked, fingering the love beads he wore around his neck.

"In fact, it would break up the routine in a big way—like, inspire us," Jack said firmly. He turned to Fi. "Remember the sign we saw on the way into town?"

"The carnival?" Fi asked.

"Exactly!" Jack declared. "Now, that would be fun *and* educational. A field trip to a carnival—you could come, too!"

"He could?" Clu made a face.

"I *could* . . ." Ned drawled. "To see exactly how 'educational' a carnival can be." He looked from Clu to Fi, to Jack. "Educate me on exactly how a carnival is educational—last I heard, field trips are usually to the zoo, or museums, or . . ."

"Local cultural events," Fi contributed.

"Like we can see how the locals have fun. . . ." Jack added.

Clu rubbed his hands together and chuckled. "Bet there's some cute chicks, too."

Jack elbowed Clu hard. Clu grunted. "Hey, dude, what's that about?"

Ned threw up his hands in a gesture of defeat. A smile spread across his face. "Okay, okay. You guys win. I don't have time for this craziness. I gotta help unload and get this crew shaped up. I don't know what's tougher sometimes, trying to educate you kids, or keeping these guys in line." Ned pocketed his glasses, and tucked his books and some papers under his arm. Heading toward the front of the bus, he added over his shoulder, "Let's bag it for today. But don't get the wrong idea. The carnival's cool for now, but I expect your homework, done . . . completely and *well*—" Ned looked at Clu—"tomorrow."

"All right!" Fi, Jack, and Clu shouted in unison. Clu slapped Jack five, then Jack said, "Hey, let's get our stuff and head out of here before he changes his mind."

"More like come to my senses!" Ned grumbled, giving Clu an affectionate shove. "Hey, Billy, not over there!" Ned broke off to shout to one of the roadies. The guy was carrying one of Molly's acoustic guitar cases. "Put that in her hotel room. . . ." Ned hurried over to talk to Billy.

"See ya, Ned!" Jack said, steering Clu toward the front of the bus. Turning to Fi, Jack added, "One problem with our plan."

"What?" Fi asked.

"Money. Carnivals aren't much fun unless you have some cash."

"Whoa, man." Clu groaned, then turned out the pockets of his jeans. "I'm broke."

"Same here." Jack cast a sheepish glance at Fi. "I sort of went overboard and spent the last of my stash on those *Blue Jivers* CDs at the Swing Festival."

Fi made a face. "Okay, guys, I'm cool for it. I've got some money back in my room. But you'll owe me." Turning back toward the bus, she slammed right into her mother. They both staggered backward, and Molly steadied Fi. Fi looked up at her mom. Molly Phillips wore a big wide smile, but had a questioning look on her face.

"Hey!" Molly said, holding Fi by her upper arms.

"Hey!" Fi said, laughing up at her mother, wondering briefly if her mom knew how great she looked; even after spending half the night on the bus writing songs, her brown eyes were bright, her cheeks pink. Molly was petite and on the thin side with high cheekbones and a complexion to die for. Dressed in black jeans and a long-sleeved black T-shirt, she looked more like Fi's older sister than her mom. Fi impulsively hugged her.

"Where are you rushing off to?" Molly asked. She glanced around, then spotted Ned helping unload the guitars from the truck. "Short school day?"

"Yeah—" Jack said. "We're going on a field trip."

Molly swept back her silky hair and frowned at Jack. "A field trip?"

Jack flashed his most charming smile at his mom. Molly didn't look impressed as he explained, "You know, change of pace and all that . . ."

Just then Irene Bell hurried up, Molly's Filofax in her hand. Irene flashed a small, absent smile. She was in her all-business mode. Being Molly's band manager was not easy, but Irene was great at keeping her organized and on track. "Molly, we're not done with this. . . ."

"Right," she said to Irene. "You kids wait a

minute . . . So, Irene, where were we?"

"You were talking about the mikes in the club," Irene reminded.

"Right . . . first, you tell the owner of that club that those mikes are *not* what's in the contract—I want all fifty-sixes."

Irene noted that in her book, then shook her head. "That guy's a crook!"

"Mom—" Fi interrupted, impatiently. "If we're ever going to get there . . ."

Molly put a hand on Fi's shoulder. "What's the big rush? The carnival isn't going anywhere—at least not today. Let me finish up with Irene."

Irene cleared her throat. "Wasn't there something about the speakers or . . ."

Molly snapped her fingers. "Right, the bass subwoofers are *way* too small. I can get more bottom end out of a car stereo."

Irene shook her head in dismay. "And you said earlier, the main PA amp is three hundred watts less than what we need. I'd better get on this right away."

Irene started over toward the club. "Oh, I almost forgot, you still want to go shopping?"

"You bet!" Molly confirmed. "How about it, Fi? I've got a few things to tie up here, then I've got a couple of hours before rehearsal. Want to hit the mall? Or even better, I thought maybe we could check out that retro clothing store—with the cute name—"

"Rethreads!" Irene laughed. "It was right at this end of Main Street. We could take the truck and be there in a flash."

For a minute Fi was torn—she loved clothes shopping with her mom. Still the carnival was sure to be more fun, more excitement. "Not today, Mom. Next time. What are you shopping for?"

"New stage clothes."

Irene put her hands together in a prayerful gesture. "Nothing black . . . please."

"Only black—" Molly insisted. "I thought something black, slinky, velvet . . ."

Irene shook her head, and Fi chuckled.

"It's not going to work, Irene," Fi warned her. Irene's campaign to turn Molly on to bright colors was doomed to failure.

"Even your pajamas are black. If there was an eclipse, you'd disappear."

"Speaking of disappearing, man, we should be making our getaway now!" Clu chimed in, jumping down the front steps of the bus. "Before my dad changes his mind."

"Okay, Mom?" Fi inquired.

"Thanks for asking." Molly laughed. "But keep in touch, okay?"

"Sure thing!" Jack assured.

"Got your pagers on?"

"That's a big ten-four! Bye, Mom!" Jack waved, taking Fi's elbow and steering her toward the bus entrance. "Time to raid your piggy bank, sis," he said under his breath.

Chapter Three

Tinny strains of a country tune blared out of the speaker that hung over the carnival ticket booth. Like the ramshackle booth, the speaker had sure seen better days, Fi guessed, putting her change and a strip of amusement ride tickets in her knapsack. The white paint on the booth was peeling; the speaker vibrated every time the lead vocalist hit a high note.

"Let's hit the fairway," Clu urged. Pocketing the five-dollar bill Fi handed him, he stopped at the turnstile at the entrance gate. He looked back over his shoulder at Fi and Jack, and exclaimed, "Are you ready for this or what!" In the sunlight his blue eyes shone brightly. "Come on, dudes, let's get going before we miss all the fun."

Fi laughed and joined Clu. "It's not even that busy yet," she pointed out, gesturing toward the main fairway. Red-and-white striped tents alternated with game and vendor booths. Although it was a weekday afternoon, attendance looked pretty respectable, but the place appeared far from crowded.

"Things won't start hopping around here until school's out," the ticket taker predicted, as first Clu, then Jack, then Fi pushed through the metal turnstile. Fi had never seen such a big carnival.

"I'm surprised the band's already playing." Jack pointed toward a small bandstand. Rows of folding chairs, filled mainly with senior citizens, ringed a portable dance floor. Some couples were dancing to the slow country waltz.

The ticket taker shrugged. "Just to warm up— themselves and the crowd. They play the bandstand during the day for church groups, and whoever's around, but tonight they open for the headliners in town from The Grand Ole Opry."

Just inside the carnival grounds, Fi stopped to study the scene. "Let's see," she said. "There's a really cool House of Glass over there." She pointed just past the Ferris wheel. "But right now I'm more in the mood for rides. How about it, guys?" Fi looked first to the left of the fairway, where she stood, then to the right. "Okay, we got the roller coaster, the Ferris wheel, the Tilt-A-Whirl . . . sort of hard to choose. Any ideas? I'm game for anything." A chorus of shrieks coming from the direction of the roller coaster caught her attention. "So, guys, what . . ." Fi faced the boys. Jack and Clu were fixated on something farther down the fairway. "Like, Jack?" Fi repeated. "I said, what do you want to check out first?"

"Her!" both boys chorused.

"Her?" Fi followed their gaze. It took a second but then Fi noticed the girl. The crowd was thin but she would have stood out in mob of about a million. She was a tall, leggy redhead in snug-fitting jeans, and had a complexion Fi would kill for. Her skin was—Fi didn't know the right word for it—sort of see-through. Talk about that inner glow, she thought enviously. The girl looked around and almost seemed to catch the guys ogling her. With a half smile, she rounded the corner of the Volunteer Firemen's Barbecue tent. Fi watched as she ambled slowly toward the games area.

Fi looked at Jack and Clu. They both had a very familiar goofy expression on their faces. "I don't believe this!" she exclaimed in exasperation. "We came to the carnival to hang out together, not to—"

"Don't you love that red hair?" Jack marveled, interrupting Fi midsentence.

"Tell me about it, dude. I feel like I'm in a shampoo commercial," Clu answered.

"C'mon, guys, she's just a girl," Fi pointed out, tapping her foot. She couldn't believe this was happening again. In the past two months Jack and Clu had become totally, incredibly *girl-crazy*. No other word for it. Whatever. From the looks of *that* girl they didn't stand a chance. She was too glamorous, too old. A senior in high school, at least. Seventeen, maybe eighteen. "Let's go try that roller coaster," Fi insisted, trying to bring them to their senses.

Jack was already too far gone. "I feel like I need to play games." He edged over to a Vintage Car Association booth and stooped slightly to check his reflection in one of the shiny hubcaps on display. He smoothed his hair, brushed off the front of his blue T-shirt, and grinned at Fi. "Yes, games are definitely in order." He cracked his knuckles and made the motions of hurling a baseball.

"In fact," Clu said with a wide grin, "I'm feeling very lucky." Jack started down the fairway, and Clu hurried to catch up with him.

Fi planted her hands on her hips and watched the guys head off. "Tell me this isn't happening," she muttered, then raised her voice over the general din. "Hey, wait a minute. Didn't we come here together?"

30

"Sure, but you're a big girl, sis. Enjoy yourself, just keep outta trouble!" Jack tossed back with a disarming smile.

Fi did not smile back. She glared after the boys. "I hate this!" she mumbled, and kicked at the dirt. Raising her voice, she made a megaphone with her hands and called after them. "If you guys split now, I'm going to keep all the ride tickets." Even to her own ears her threat lacked punch.

Jack and Clu didn't even bother to turn around. They were nearly jogging to try to catch up with the mystery girl.

Jack shoved his hands in his pockets and continued jauntily down the fairway away from Fi. He stifled a pang of guilt. He had pretended not to hear her, but she sounded a little lost, left out. Still . . . he couldn't spend his life—or most of this road trip—hanging with his kid sister.

"Man." Clu rested his hand on Jack's shoulder, slowing him down slightly. "What's a girl like that doing here alone?"

Before Jack could think about it, Clu added, worried, "Dude, do you think she really *is* alone? Like, what if she's meeting a guy . . ."

"We do an about-face, and find Fi," Jack said. "But she *did* give me that sort of 'hi there' look!"

"You? Dream on!" Clu snorted. "She was looking right at me!"

"No way!" Jack said, though Clu just might have been right. For some reason girls tended to find Clu cute.

Jack hadn't quite figured out what Clu's secret was. Maybe because the dude looked so helpless half the time. Pride kept him from asking Fi what girls saw in Clu. Whatever. This time around Jack was determined to win the girl.

"Anyway, she looks lonely," Clu added. "So there probably isn't some guy, maybe he stood her up!"

Lonely. Again Jack's conscience pricked him. Fi was probably lonely right now. He hated dumping her like that, but still he wished Fi had been able to have a friend come along on this road trip, the way Jack had Clu.

"'Course, you know who really looked lonely?" Clu asked, then answered himself. "Fi."

Jack looked up quickly at his friend. There he goes again, Jack thought. Clu, who sometimes seemed dense as a plank, had a way of mind reading whatever Jack was thinking. He was almost psychic—if a guy believed in that stuff. It threw Jack sometimes.

"Fi only cares about the rides," Jack tossed off. "But if you think she's lonely, you could go back and join her," he suggested wickedly. "She was heading for the roller coaster."

"No way, dude!" Clu protested. "I saw the redhead first! Anyway, like who needs a roller coaster! My heart's already in overdrive from looking at that girl. How old do you think she is?" Clu sounded worried.

Jack didn't answer. The girl had stopped on the fringe of a small crowd gathered in front of a ringtoss game. Rows of green bottles stood on a table in front of a display of prizes, mainly stuffed animals. She was focused on the game, but as Jack started toward the girl, she looked over her shoulder at him, and dazzled him with a brilliant smile.

He felt like he was snared on the end of some invisible fishing line. Her smile drew him right up to her. But Clu beat him to it. "Hi, I'm Clu!" The girl smiled benevolently at Clu.

"I'm Jack," Jack butted in quickly.

The girl turned a pair of startling turquoise-blue eyes toward him. She didn't introduce herself, but her smile widened, showing a pair of lovely dimples.

Jack smiled back, then she turned toward Clu and smiled beautifully at him.

Jack glared at Clu. Clu glared at Jack.

Before Jack could say a thing, Clu leaned toward the girl and asked, "So, are you like really here alone?"

She tilted her head slightly, and toyed with the drawstring on the neck of her red hooded sweatshirt. She met Clu's eyes a moment, then dropped her gaze, and blushed prettily.

That's a yes! Jack was sure of it. He stepped between Clu and the girl. "Nobody should have to be alone at the carnival—"

Clu tapped Jack on the chest. "You left your *sister* alone."

Jack lifted his eyebrows. "So, why don't you go hang out with her?"

"No way. I'm going to win our new friend a stuffed animal. Like stuffed animals?" Clu grinned at the girl.

She nodded.

Jack chuckled, and rubbed his hands together. "Nice try, Clu, but you *never* win at these things."

Clu sniffed. "Come off it, man. I won a gold-fish at that school fair in Missoula."

"Right, the woman gave it to you because she felt sorry for you!" Jack pulled a sad face. "And he didn't feed it, either." Jack was surprised at the girl's reaction. Girls usually got weepy about stuff like dead goldfish. At least Fi usually did.

The girl continued to smile a kind of far-off smile. "'Course on the road, the way we live with the *band*, its hard to have a pet," Jack added, hoping to pique the girl's interest. Girls loved rock musicians.

Maybe she'd think Clu and he were musicians. Or roadies.

Clu pulled some money out of his pocket and handed it to the man behind the ringtoss booth. The man's forearms were covered with tattoos, and muscles bulged beneath his white T-shirt. "Twelve rings please."

"Okay, guys," the attendant said, flashing a crooked smile. Jack noticed two of his front teeth were missing.

Clue turned to Jack and smiled. "Okay, ol' buddy, time to put your money where your mouth is."

"Better believe it," Jack said defiantly. "Same

for me," he told the attendant, plunking down his money.

"You're going down!" Clu predicted, and rubbed one of the rings against his shirt. "Here goes!"

Jack folded his arms, stood back a little, and watched the girl watch Clu. Clu Frisbee'd one hoop after another in the general direction of the bottle. "Whoa!" Jack guffawed, as each of Clu's rings sailed wide of their mark, landing on the floor of the booth next to the attendant.

The girl laughed, too, silently, putting her hand over her mouth. Her skin was so fair, so delicate, Jack could see the blue of her veins on the back of her hand. "Hey," he asked, dropping his voice, "what did you say your name was?" The girl didn't answer; she returned Jack's gaze, and her lips lifted in another small secret smile that made Jack's heart skip an alarming number of beats.

Chapter Four

"**P**athetic. Perfectly pathetic!" Fi grumbled as she skirted a crowd of preschoolers lined up at the entrance to the carousel. How could Clu and Jack just abandon her like that?

Fi couldn't care less about their obsession with girls. She shook her head. Some girls—seriously *brain-challenged* girls, in Fi's personal opinion— thought Clu in particular was cute.

Personally, she wasn't really interested in guys that way yet. But even if she were, she'd never walk out on her *friends*, or her own brother, and leave them alone at a carnival. No guy would be worth that. She felt betrayed.

Without much enthusiasm, Fi traveled the dirt walkway leading from the carousel, past the Ferris wheel. Ferris wheels bored her.

But the Tilt-A-Whirl, farther down the ride arcade, looked seriously scary—at the moment its red-blue-and-yellow disk was spinning perpendicular to the ground, and riders sitting strapped into their spinning metal cages were emitting wonderfully earsplitting shrieks.

Problem was, sometimes Tilt-A-Whirls bothered Fi's stomach, which at the moment was in a knot.

But, roller coasters—even a major case of the flu couldn't keep Fi off a roller coaster. To her left, across from a kiddie pony ride, towered an extremely high roller coaster. A huge sign hanging across the framework of the ride read THE CATACLYSM.

Looks like a good scary ride, Fi decided, studying the roller coaster from behind the chain-link fence blocking the ride off from the fairway. The first slow climb, practically perpendicular to the sky, was followed by a steep immediate drop, then lots of wild curves and plunges. Jack would love this, she thought, knowing how he and Clu would have fought with Fi to ride in the front seat.

Well, this was one time Jack would have to miss out on the fun. Though, Fi wondered, what kind of fun was riding a roller coaster alone? Fi kicked at the dirt and took a deep breath. Well, she was on her own, and there was not much she could do about it. At least she was in the possession of *all* the tickets to the amusement rides. Maybe she would use every one of them herself.

Tugging down the long sleeves of her pale purple shirt, Fi marched up to the roller coaster and planted herself at the end of a line of middle-school kids. Everyone was in pairs or groups of three or four. Fi tried not to notice. She pulled out her strip of tickets and tore off four. She adored roller coasters and would ride four times straight through, mentally deducting three of the tickets from Clu and Jack's allotment.

The line shuffled forward. Fi wondered if the other kids noticed she was the only person alone. People probably thought she was some kind of geek or nerd who didn't have a friend in the world.

Fi fought back the tears that pressed right behind her eyes. Running her fingers along the chain-link fence that surrounded the roller coaster, she vowed she would not let Clu or Jack make her cry over this.

She took a deep breath. Maybe planning revenge would take her mind off feeling lonely. She tried to picture a suitable punishment—unstringing Jack's guitar and hiding the strings somewhere strange, like in the freezer.

As for Clu—Fi tried to conjure up a particularly evil way to get back at him. Suddenly she felt like she was glued to the ground. She looked down and lifted her foot. One end of a thick wad of pink gum was on the ground, the other end was stuck to the sole of her sneaker. "I don't believe this," she groaned.

A kid behind her giggled. "That's beyond yucky!"

Fi whirled around. "Whatever, it's not your business," she barked unreasonably.

"Hey, it's not like *I* put it there." The girl tossed her ponytail and snapped back at Fi.

"No, *you* didn't," Fi softened her tone and felt beyond embarrassed as she scraped the sole of her sneaker against the fence trying to get the gum off. "I'm sorry," she mumbled, but inside she was still seething. Somehow the day was zooming from bad to worse, and it all felt like Jack and Clu's fault.

Have I lost my magic touch or what? Clu wondered. They'd been hanging out with the girl for at least forty-five minutes, maybe more, and still she hadn't said a single word.

After the ringtoss, Clu and Jack had each tried their hand at one of those swing-the-hammer-and-ring-the-bell games. Clu had scored "major wimp"; Jack had done better, but not much: he had scored "beginning feather lifter." That hadn't done much to impress that girl, and Clu was beginning to wonder.

"Hey, Jack, is she, like, beyond shy, or what?" Clu asked softly, as they strolled down the fairway a few steps behind the girl.

"Maybe," Jack conceded, "but she seems to like being with us."

True, Clu thought as they continued toward the next games area. "Hey, are those baseballs I see before me?!" Clu exclaimed, his heart lifting. He slowed down in front of a booth.

It was decorated with a circus theme. Bright balloons and garlands of fake popcorn festooned the front of the gaily painted stall. Colorful drawings of tightrope walkers, and lion tamers and acrobats framed the sides of the stand. Rows of clown faces had been painted on a board, and in the middle of each face was a hole surrounded by a bright red clown's mouth.

"Come on, fellas." The guy behind the booth shoved back his red baseball cap and pointed right at Clu. "Win your girl's heart by winning one of these humongous, class A-1 stuffed animals. Just land three baseballs in a clown's mouth and the biggest, most enticing prize will be yours."

Now, baseball was something Clu was good at, though he was more of a slugger than a pitcher. Still—

"Ball toss!" Jack nodded. "I could go for that." The girl turned, arching her eyebrows.

"You game for this?" Clu asked her. She bit her lower lip and nodded eagerly, her eyes drifting to the top shelf, where the largest stuffed toys were displayed: giant pandas, four-foot-high giraffes, a huge lion, and several enormous elephants in assorted colors.

The carnie juggled the balls invitingly at the boys.

The girl looked from the giant panda back at Clu. Inspired to make those baby blues shine even brighter, Clu reached in his pocket and pulled out his last single. "Three balls please," he ordered.

"Three here," Jack piped up, counting out a fistful of quarters.

Clu rolled the first ball between his hands, then wound up and hurled the ball toward the mouth of the center clown. *THWACK!* It rebounded off the board and sailed under the front of the booth.

"Oooooh." Jack ducked dramatically and covered his eyes.

"Not so hard," the attendant prompted. "Your aim was good."

Looking across Clu's chest directly at the girl, Jack laughed. "At least he didn't hit me!"

The girl covered her mouth with her hand and stifled a giggle.

"Laugh your heart out, Jack," Clu challenged, and hurled his second ball. This one landed short of the backstop. Before Jack could comment, Clu picked up his last ball.

"This is the one. C'mon, lucky number three." Pitching underhanded this time, he actually landed the ball on the edge of the clown's mouth. It teetered a moment before rolling out onto the ground. "Oh!" Clu wailed, and jammed his hands in his pockets.

"Don't feel bad," Jack comforted in a smug voice. "Not *every* man is meant to be a great pitcher. Now." He turned to the girl. She was watching him, wide-eyed. "Watch a pro at work!"

"You, a *pro*!" Clu made barfing noises.

"Don't listen to him," Jack directed to the girl. "All right, for the stuffed tiger . . ." Jack's throw went wide, right outside of the booth. The ball slowly rolled down the slight grade alongside the booth, landing at Clu's feet.

"Aaaaggh!" Jack groaned, then quickly hurled his last two balls—again his throws went wide of their mark.

Clu began to gloat. Like the carnie had said, don't throw too hard. "I've got it figured out!" he crowed. "All I need is three more balls." Bringing his face close to Jack's, he warned, "Watch and weep!" Clu felt in his pockets. "Darn! Hey, man." He dropped his voice and leaned in toward Jack. "I need to borrow some money."

Jack shook his head slightly. "So, old pal, what happened to 'Watch and weep'?"

"C'mon, man, as a friend."

"Fi's fund just ran out, 'friend.' I'm flat broke, too."

"Bummer!" Clu remarked. He flashed a sheepish smile at the girl. She smiled back. That inspired Clu. "Okay, plan B. Make conversation."

Clu leaned back with his elbows against the counter of the ball-toss kiosk. Noticing the logo on the girl's sweatshirt, he read the words over the picture of a bear aloud. "Bardo High!" Clu nodded approvingly. The girl was still in high school, or had graduated recently enough that she wasn't embarrassed to wear a school shirt. Maybe she wasn't as old as she looked. "So lemme guess, the Bardo Bears are the high school football team, right?"

The girl mugged a silly face.

"Guess that was pretty lame," Clu admitted good-naturedly. The girl shrugged and consoled him with a smile.

"That's the only bummer about going to school on the road," Jack remarked. "No teams."

"Not!" Clu interjected. "We have a kind of team thing going."

"What team thing?" Jack asked.

"Like the Band versus the Roadies on bowling nights, dude." He explained to the girl, "He'd like to forget about it all. 'Cause his mom's in the band, so he's on the band's team. My dad's a roadie, and the Roadies rule."

"No way!" Jack protested loudly. "The Band is king of the league!"

"In your dreams! You're lucky to get spares!" said Clu.

"Who was the one that got his fingers stuck in the ball?" Jack reminded Clu, turning his back on the girl.

"It was a rental ball! Who slipped on the alley trying to be all fancy with his follow-through?" Clu accused.

"Hey!" Jack suddenly grabbed Clu's arm. "Where's she going?" He pointed behind Clu's back. Clu whirled around. The girl was hurrying through the crowd, as if she had suddenly remembered she had to be somewhere.

Clu complained. "Now look what you did!"

"*Me!*" Jack tapped his own chest. "You're kidding right? You're the one who wanted to make conversation!" He made a disgusted sound, then marched right past Clu. The girl was walking quickly away. "Hey, wait up—I don't even know your name!"

"Me neither!" Clu said, jogging to keep up with Jack. But the girl didn't seem to hear them. She continued toward the amusement rides, her back toward the carnival entrance and the House of Mirrors. She disappeared behind the Volunteer Firemen's Barbecue tent.

"We lost her!" Clu cried, as he and Jack rounded the corner of the large food stand. "Well, *I'm* not giving up!" Jack said and continued down the fairway. "She should be easy to spot, even in this crowd."

* * *

"EEEEEEEEEEEEEEE!" The gleeful shriek rang shrilly in Fi's ear as the roller coaster cars plunged down the final steep drop of The Cataclysm. Fi was alone in the front seat. She had her arms folded across her chest. Maybe if I could give a good loud scream, I'd feel better, she thought. Venting her anger at Jack and Clu would probably be a good idea.

But Fi was too mad even to scream. As the cars rattled around the final, slow curve, pulled back into the starting shed, and yanked to a halt, Fi thought, Maybe I'll just tell Mom. But as Fi climbed out, she knew she'd never tell Molly. She hated being a snitch.

Fi started back toward the game area. She cut through the small paths between the tents sheltering the little kid rides. She couldn't imagine that the guys were still flirting with that girl, but the colorful row of game kiosks was as good a place as any to find them.

"Hey, there she is!" Jack's exclamation floated over the general din of the crowd.

"Wait up!" Clu's voice called out.

Fi looked up. "I don't believe it!" She didn't see Clu or Jack, but the girl they'd been chasing was heading right down the path toward Fi. Her face wore a worried look, and she was walking quickly, her head down.

"Hey!" Fi called as the girl approached her. The girl looked up, and met Fi's eyes. Up close the girl was even prettier than Fi remembered. Fi smiled tentatively, as the girl continued toward her. "Sorry if my brother and his friend have been—" Fi broke off. The girl was heading straight for her. "Hey, watch out . . ." Fi gasped as the girl held her glance and continued walking directly toward Fi.

One minute the girl was face-to-face with Fi, only inches away; the next minute she marched right into her.

All at once Fi's whole body shuddered violently, and an icy current coursed up her spine, down her legs and arms, and into her toes and fingertips. The tingling sensation intensified until Fi felt light-headed—as if she were going to faint. She reached out her hands to grab on to the girl to steady herself. But instead of closing on the fabric of the girl's red sweatshirt, Fi's hands closed on thin air.

Just when Fi thought she might collapse, the feeling stopped as quickly as it started. She turned around just in time to see the girl still walking quickly down the fairway. But even as Fi watched, the girl's whole body began to shimmer.

Right before Fi's eyes, the girl grew more and more transparent, until she faded away completely.

Chapter Five

"**H**ey, sis, did you see her?" Jack asked, rushing up and grabbing Fi's arm. "That girl with the red hair and the red sweatshirt—the one we followed?"

Jack's touch grounded Fi, bringing her back to the present. It was as if for ten seconds or so the world had stopped for Fi. Now from behind her she heard the hurdy-gurdy tunes of the merry-go-round, the cries of vendors barking their wares, and she inhaled the fragrance of french fries and sweet sugar-coated nuts in the air. It was as if Fi had just come back to life from . . . from . . . what or where she wasn't sure.

That girl walked right through me! was Fi's next thought. It was another second before she found her voice. She stared down the fairway and kept pointing to where she'd last seen the girl.

"Where'd she go, man?" Clu wondered, rushing up.

"Who knows?" Fi finally managed to answer. "One minute she was here, and the next . . . she just vanished."

"I knew it, dude! She was too good to be true. There had to be some other guy in her life—probably a whole football team of other guys!" Clu exclaimed, pounding his fist in his hand. "She checked her watch or something and remembered the big date. BMOC, I bet."

"No, Clu!" Fi contradicted him with a firm shake of her head. "I'm telling you, she disappeared."

Jack snorted and shot Clu a look of pure disgust. "The way *he* makes conversation, I can understand. I'd beat a hasty exit myself."

Fi made Jack face her. "Not like split the scene, Jack. I mean literally."

Jack snickered. "Poof! She sees psychic you and just evaporates. Gimme a break, Fi!"

Fi ignored Jack's jibe. "I'm not kidding, Jack. She sort of—I don't know." Fi searched for the right word. "She just walked up to me—through me—like I didn't exist, and when I turned around she was hurrying down the fairway. I could see through her, then she disappeared completely."

"Not as in 'swallowed by the crowd'!" Jack remarked, folding his arms across his chest and looking at Fi like she'd sprouted three heads or something.

Clu gawked at Fi. "What are you trying to tell us? She was a ghost?" He sounded awed.

"Here we go," Jack mumbled, half under his breath. Heaving a sigh, he explained in a patient tone, "Fi, this is not the time for one of your way-out theories."

Fi decided to ignore the fact he was talking to her like she was a three-year-old. She shrugged. "I know what I saw."

"I know what *we* saw," Jack countered instantly. "Don't you think we would have noticed if she were some kind of disembodied soul? She was a living, breathing girl. I mean, we talked to her for half an hour."

"Who did the talking? She or you?" Fi folded her arms across her chest and looked from Jack to Clu, back to Jack again.

Jack frowned.

Fi permitted herself a smug sense of satisfaction. She tapped her foot impatiently. "Well, what did she say? After a half hour, you should at least know her name."

"Her name, right." Clu sounded miserable. "Y'know, Fi's got a point, Jack."

Jack lifted his shoulders. "No, we never did find out her name," he admitted slowly. "We were too busy trying to win her a prize. And we did the talking, but she never got much of a chance to say anything. Clu, as usual, kept interrupting."

Clu's eyes widened. "I did?"

"You kept contradicting everything I said. Trying to act like Big Man on Campus or something," Jack accused.

"*Me?!*" Clu planted his hands on his hips. "You're the one who was bragging about being the world's champion bowler or something. . . ."

"Enough!" Fi raised her voice and made a calming gesture with both her hands. "I get Jack's drift," she added, brushing her bangs out of her eyes. "No girl in her right mind is going to hang around listening to you two try to one-up each other. But that's not the point."

"That's all that matters to me," Jack said, casting a wistful glance down the fairway toward the entrance gate. "She's gone."

"At least we agree on that," Fi said. "So even though you guys tried to chat her up, she never even told you her name." Clu nodded in agreement, and Fi went on. "She never said a thing to you." Fi tried to put her thoughts in order. "Think. Did either one of you actually touch her?"

Clu gasped. "Hey, what kind of guys do you

think we are? We'd just met the girl. It wasn't even a first date!"

"Get real, Clu, I'm not accusing you of acting inappropriately," Fi said impatiently. "But you know it's only natural to touch her sweater, brush against her."

"Whatever, I don't remember touching her at all," Jack said. "Believe me, I would. But she did have a kind of hands-off quality about her I sort of liked, actually," Jack said dreamily. "Just like I would have liked the chance to ask her out on a date."

"Over my dead body!" Clu protested.

"Sorry, guys. I hate to tell you this, but if she did go out with either of you, it would be your first date with a doppelgänger."

"Fi, not again!" Jack made a small sound of disgust. "Everything that happens lately you blame on ghosts or ghouls or something . . . this girl was not a ghost. She was a flesh-and-blood, very attractive chick, who as much as I hate to admit it, probably just had better things to do than hang with two cool guys like us."

"Yeah, right," Fi said with derision. "And that's not fair to say I blame everything on ghouls—unless it was two ghouls who dumped me at the entrance to this carnival to chase after some *dream* girl," she added pointedly.

She slowly began walking toward the entrance, picking her way through the growing crowd and thinking aloud as she went. "But why would a ghost hang out here?"

"You're really serious," Clu remarked, and gave a little shiver. "Like she was the undead, or something. What are girls called who lure guys to their graves?" Clu looked around.

Fi patted his arm. "I'm sure she wasn't luring you anywhere," she reassured him. "But why here, why at a carnival?" Fi stopped and searched the crowd, her gaze traveling from the booths to the rides to the very ordinary looking long barns where animal exhibits and 4-H club contests were being held. "Unless these grounds are built on the site of an old graveyard."

Clu picked up his feet quickly, one after the other, as if he were walking on hot coals.

"Clu, don't tell me you're falling for this weirdness!" Jack cried.

"Well, it sort of makes sense. She didn't say one word to us, Jack!"

"Maybe she's just shy. Who knows what her problem is?" Jack stopped and pointed toward a french fry stand. "But I know what my major problem right now is. I can't think with an empty stomach. The little gray cells in the brain are shriveling for lack of french fries." He grinned at Fi. "Hey, sis, if you got a couple of more bucks I'll treat us to some fries. Then we'll go try to find the girl."

"How can you think of food at a time like this?" Clu clutched at his heart. "The girl of my dreams is a ghost, and you're thinking of your stomach."

Fi was still trying to puzzle the whole thing out. Absently she reached in her pocket and handed Jack a five-dollar bill.

"Hey, and soda, too!" Jack cheered, starting toward the french fry vendor.

"Or maybe," Fi figured aloud, "maybe there was a freak accident at a carnival here in the past."

"She didn't look like she was from the past," said Clu, as Jack walked up with a large tub of french fries and an extra-large soda.

"Nor did she look *dead*. Come off it, Clu, Fi's gone over the top again." Jack offered Fi some fries, put a hand on her shoulder, and looked her in the eye. She read the concern in his face and sighed, bracing herself for a "be sensible" lecture.

"Fi, she was not a ragged-looking ghost. She was a real girl, wearing a real Bardo High Bears sweatshirt for Pete's sake."

"Bardo High," Fi repeated, slowly munching on a fry. "But didn't she seem too old for high school?"

"Beats me," Clu piped up. "I'd say seventeen, eighteen. Maybe nineteen," he added sadly. "Probably too old for us."

"So she's probably already graduated." Fi grew thoughtful. "But she still was wearing that sweatshirt," she said, brightening. "And that gives me an idea!"

Fi impulsively hugged Clu. "Remind me I'm still mad at you two, but thanks, Clu!" With that she hurried toward the turnstile. She shot back over her shoulder. "Sometimes, Clu Bell, you are a real genius!"

"Me?!" Clu's jaw dropped.

"You do have your moments." Jack laughed, clapping his pal on the back, then yelled after Fi, "Hey, where are you going?"

"Why, Bardo High, of course!" she exclaimed, pushing through the turnstile. Fi stopped to ask the ticket taker where the school was.

"Wait for me!" Jack shouted, barreling through the turnstile.

"Me, too!" Clu jogged up. "I saw her first!"

"You?!" Jack scoffed, as they fell in step with Fi.

"Yeah, me, and besides, I think she likes me better!"

"Whatever, you two," Fi said. "If we want to get to Bardo High before school's out for the day, we'd better stop gabbing, and walk fast. According to that guy at the ticket booth, it's about a forty-minute walk from here." With that, Fi made a right turn at the corner and hurried down the leaf-strewn sidewalk back toward Main Street.

Chapter Six

BARDO HIGH
Home of the Bardo Bears

The white sign hung between two metal poles at the entrance to the modern brick-faced school building. A cute logo of a grizzly bear wearing a Bardo High sweatshirt and carrying a football tucked neatly under one arm decorated the sign.

Students streamed down the front steps, onto the broad walkway, and across the lawn. Clumps of kids headed for the parking lot and school buses. A chorus of cheers and shouts wafted from the direction of the playing fields. For a moment all three kids stopped to watch.

"Almost makes you miss going to a real school," Clu remarked, looking around.

"Can't believe *you* of all people said that." Jack laughed. "Though I do miss being on some sort of sports team."

"And meeting cheerleaders!"

"Well, you guys can keep ogling those cheerleaders, but I'm heading inside before the library closes. Obviously school's out for the day, and I want to check out that girl you two were supposedly so in love with," Fi teased.

With mixed emotions, she hurried up the front steps of the school. She hadn't been in a school building since last June, just before they started the tour. She'd always adored school, though she was careful not to admit that to too many of her friends. Certainly not to Jack or Clu. She didn't want them to add one more item to their "Fi is a dork!" list. Bad enough she was hooked on computers, cyberspace, science, and all things weird. But she truly did love school, and as she entered the crowded foyer of Bardo High, she felt a pang of regret that this fall was the first time since she was five that she hadn't had the great first-day-back-at-school feeling, the smell of the new textbooks, a new loose-leaf binder, a pencil case filled with new pencils, pens, and erasers. A class full of mainly familiar but some new faces. Possible new friends.

"The library's that way!" Jack pointed down a corridor to the left. Double glass doors at the end of the hall stood open. Just inside was a desk with a sign: RETURNS/CHECKOUTS HERE.

Fi marched through the doors and looked for a librarian. The room was fairly empty, though some of the study carrels were occupied, and a couple of kids were goofing around in front of the book-locating computer.

She spotted a student pushing a library cart behind the returns counter. The cart was stacked high with books. The boy angled the cart near a computer terminal, and began scanning each book before moving them to another cart.

Approaching him with a big smile, Fi noticed the name tag pinned to his polo shirt. "Hi, Dan," she greeted him.

He looked up, his expression nervous. He was having a severely bad skin day, and Fi instantly saw he was shy. She figured him to be about fifteen.

"Do you know me?" Dan asked, backing away from Fi slightly.

Fi tried not to laugh. "Uh, no. I thought since you worked here you could help me."

"Oh," he said flatly, and relaxed a little. "I'll try."

From behind her, Fi heard Jack heave a sigh. She reached back and pinched his wrist. *Please can the smart remarks, bro.* She wished she were really psychic so she could download her thoughts directly into his sometimes thick brain.

Fi focused back on Dan. "This is going to sound kind of weird, but I'm trying to find a girl who I think used to go to school here."

Dan's dark eyebrows drew together. "I-I don't know about that. I'm not supposed to give out student information—not that I have any." He shot a glance at the computer as if he were afraid somehow Fi might make him access some secret student record file. "No. Actually that's not something I can help you with. If the librarian were here, she—"

"But if she isn't?" Fi shrugged. "Aren't you in charge?"

"Me?" He met Fi's gaze with amazed green eyes. "I'm just a student, y'know." He dropped his gaze and went back to scanning books.

"This is getting us nowhere fast," Jack grumbled softly.

Fi put her hand up in warning. She cleared her throat, then leaned across the counter and looked Dan squarely in the face.

"I admire your integrity, but I'm only in town till tomorrow and I could really, really use your help."

Dan met Fi's glance. Fi tried to smile her most pathetic smile. Dan sighed. "I really don't have access to student records, but," he added slowly, "there's another way."

"Man, I feel like I'm in some kind of double-oh-seven flick!" Clu whispered to Jack.

"All this intrigue is driving me nuts," Jack grumbled. "All we're looking for is the name of a girl."

Fi turned and glared at Jack. "Will you keep quiet!" she whispered fiercely.

Dan reached under the counter and put up a little sign saying BACK IN 5 MINUTES. He motioned Fi to follow him toward the bookshelves on the right side of the room.

They passed several sets of large picture windows looking out on a soccer field and the small football stadium. Then Dan led them to the last shelf at the end of the aisle.

"So what's her name?" he asked.

"We don't know. But she had dark auburn hair—" Fi said.

Jack interrupted. "Sort of wavy, curly, and she's really pretty. A standout."

Clu added, "Very cool-looking."

Dan chuckled. "That could be half the kids here. Anyway, what makes you say she used to go here?"

Fi answered. "She looked like she's eighteen or even a bit older, like she's in college now.

Anyway she was wearing a Bardo High sweatshirt with a bear on it."

"If it had a bear on it, she went here sometime in the last five years." He pulled several large books off a shelf. "These are yearbooks." He handed them around to Fi, Clu, and Jack.

"Before we were the Bears, we used to be called the Bardo Fighting Ferrets," Dan explained. "But our team got made fun of so much they changed it to the Bears. If she went here, she'd be in one of these."

"This could take hours!" Jack remarked, settling down at a nearby empty table. Fi and Clu took the other two chairs.

"Skip to the upperclassmen photos in each book, otherwise it *will* take you hours. Every junior and senior has a picture taken," Dan said. Fi nodded. She started with the first book Dan handed her. Quickly she turned the pages of pictures. "Nope, not here," she said, reaching for another book.

"Sort of like looking through mug shots," Clu grumbled, closing his book.

"Lots of nice-looking girls," Jack remarked, turning the pages of his book more slowly. "But not *the* girl."

"Maybe you guys didn't get a good enough look at her," Dan said to Fi. "If she ever went here, she'd be in one of these books."

"Believe me, we got a very good look at her," Jack told Dan.

"Yeah, we spent half the afternoon with her," Clu added wistfully, picking up another book on the table.

"And you don't know her name?" Dan sounded skeptical. "Good luck. I've got to dig into that pile of returns over there, before the librarian gets miffed. I'll come back to check in on you guys later. You need more help, you know where to find me," he concluded. He shoved his hands in the pockets of his khakis and strolled off.

"This is the last one, unless you find something, Clu," Jack said a few minutes later. He tossed the yearbook on the pile with the others. "Now that I know just about every Bardo High alumnus, I can't wait till the ten-year reunion to see how everyone's changed."

Fi chuckled. "Or to see what predictions came true! I've read at least five different blurbs saying someone was sure to be president of the United States!"

"Or 'most likely to succeed'!" Jack added. "But

this has sure been one waste of time," he concluded, pushing back his chair.

"Or maybe not, dude!" Clu cried excitedly. He brandished a yearbook dated the June before. He held open a page and tapped a photo with one finger. "This is her! I'm sure of it!"

"No way!" Jack gasped. "That girl's a real loser." He tapped at the photo. "Look at her."

"I wouldn't say she looks like a loser. Though she looks younger than in person, a *lot* younger."

Fi felt a wave of sympathy. The face staring up at her from the page wore a sad, distant expression. Everything about the girl in the picture seemed lifeless. As if the spirit had been washed out of her. Even her hair, which was so gloriously full and shiny in person, hung sort of limp. She wore no makeup, and though she was not unattractive, no one would think she was gorgeous. Not the sort of girl that guys would follow down the fairway at a carnival, Fi reflected, puzzled.

"Not a babe, for sure!" Clu said, disappointed. "But I'm positive it's her. Look at those eyes."

"I'm with you Clu. That's the same girl, except she looks like she's had a makeover since this photo was taken," Fi said, then began to read the caption beneath the picture. "'Claire Avner. Math

Society, Science Club, Honor Roll . . .' Sounds like she was a lock for valedictorian. I wonder what happened to her."

"To who?" Dan sauntered up, a stack of books in his arms.

"We found her," Fi declared, and tapped the photo on the page. "I wonder what became of her after she left here."

"Left here?" Dan frowned.

"Yeah, after graduation!" Jack explained.

Dan gave Jack a weird look. "She's still a senior. She won't graduate until next June. I saw her when I passed the chemistry lab this afternoon. That was about an hour ago—last period. And she was perfectly fine."

Chapter Seven

The Game Charade on South Main Street was packed with the usual after-school crowd. Pinball machines lined one wall of the arcade, and a gang of kids sporting tattoos, purple hair, and nose rings hovered around one machine called Planet Buster.

The rest of the space was devoted to the latest electronic and video games. Fi lifted her voice above the general din and declared hotly, "Sorry, Jack. You're wrong. I know what I saw. That girl, Claire Avner, walked right *through* me!" She and Jack had been arguing the whole way from Bardo High about the mystery girl.

As they had headed back in the general direction of the Bardo Hotel, Jack had insisted that the girl was real, but maybe this Claire Avner was a dorky kid sister of the girl they saw at the carnival.

Fi was sure the girl in the yearbook was the very same person as the girl from the carnival.

Clu had stayed out of the conversation. He seemed let down that the yearbook blurbs made his beloved Claire sound so smart. "Would a math whiz even look at me?" He moaned. "I mean, once she saw that I was really math challenged." But halfway back to the hotel, he'd spotted the game parlor. One of Clu's goals on the road was to try every arcade in every town they stopped at. At the sight of The Game Charade, Clu brightened and dragged Jack and Fi inside to check out the scene. Claire seemed to at least temporarily slip to the back of his mind, as Clu instantly glommed on to an electronic pinball game he'd never seen before.

"I know you don't believe me," Fi continued, toying with the strap of her backpack. "But I'm not making this up, Jack. I don't lie."

"I know that." Jack softened his tone.

Frustrated, Fi chafed her arms. Every time she mentioned that Claire had walked through her, an icy current seemed to race through her veins. She wished for a minute she could trade bodies with her brother. Then he'd know she was telling the truth.

Jack absently pulled at one of the levers of the cowboy-themed pinball game. "Fi," he said in a reasonable tone, "it just doesn't add up. First of all, this Claire Avner girl is in the land of the living—"

"Yeah," Fi remarked, "but in two places at

once! We all saw her at the carnival at the same time that guy saw her in class."

"Maybe he was wrong. Maybe she cut school. Maybe he got his days mixed up. He didn't seem all that swift. Maybe he saw her last week."

"That's a lot of 'maybes,'" Fi pointed out as they strolled over toward Clu. He was in front of the electronic game, frantically working a joystick and yelling at the figures zooming across the large video screen.

"Take that, evil bumpers!" Clu shouted, then gave a cheer. "Gotcha!"

Jack made a small sound of disgust. "Clu, remember Claire. Will you focus here, man?"

"Hey, this is all about Claire. I'm busy drowning my sorrow for the lost, mysterious Claire."

"Come on, Clu," Jack urged, shaking his head. "Fi's convinced we're wrong. That the girl at the carnival wasn't real."

"But she was—even if she was in two places at once!" Clu said nonchalantly.

Jack groaned. "She wasn't in two places at once. I just told Fi that Dan must have been wrong. She cut chemistry, that's all."

"Say you're right," Fi remarked, leaning back against a column painted with garish green and yellow stripes. "Even if the person I saw was somebody else, how could she just disappear?"

"Arrgh!" Clu groaned loudly and pounded his fist on the game console. "Oh, man. Twenty thousand away from an instant replay and I get a gutter ball!" He staggered a few steps down the row of games, clutching his hand over his heart.

Jack burst out laughing. "Don't take it so hard."

Clu flashed Jack a look of pure disgust. "Don't you get it, man? This is tragic. I've loved *and* lost," he declared, then flopped onto a video game cabinet.

Fi shook her head and tried to stifle a grin. "Clu, you are beyond weird sometimes," she said; then her eye traveled past Clu's sagging shoulder. The artwork painted on the video game cabinet was amazing: a huge blue-green monster-warrior lay vanquished on a battlefield. The victorious hero held a silver sword high above his head. But the monster's ghost was shown rising from his prone body—a pale wraith of himself, arms outstretched and reaching far across a garish bloodred sky.

Fi's hands flew to her throat. "That's it!" she cried suddenly.

"What's what?" Jack responded, puzzled.

Clu answered before Fi got a chance. Shaking

his long blond hair back from his face, he exclaimed. "What *this* is, is one cool game! Another first-timer for me. Never seen this one before. Astral Monster and Sword of Stealth!" Clu fished some quarters out of his pocket and began playing the new video game.

"Fi?" Jack put his hand on her shoulder. "Answer me, what's what?"

"No time to explain now," Fi said, looking around the game room. Sure enough, back by the food vending machines was a pay phone. Digging in her pocket for a quarter, she raced back toward the phone booth.

"Who are you calling?" Jack asked, hurrying up to her. He put a hand on her wrist. "Fi, what's going on? What happened?"

"I figured it out, Jack," she declared excitedly. "That game back there. It jogged my memory. The thing I couldn't put into place back at the carnival. It's astral projection." Fi reached under the metal counter of the booth, and pulled out the Bardo phone book.

"Astral what?" Jack repeated. "What's that? Some kind of audiovisual presentation?"

Fi looked up from leafing through the phone book. "That's when people can make their spirits leave their bodies. It's kind of like becoming a ghost, except you can go back into your sleeping body afterward and wake up as if nothing happened." Fi went back to the phone book. "Cool! There are only four Avners listed."

"Fi, you're not going to start calling perfect strangers . . ." Jack objected.

Fi didn't seem to hear him. "So anyway, Jack, that explains why Claire disappeared . . . and why she never said anything! It was her astral form you guys followed at the carnival! I was reading all about this just last night. Astral bodies can float around, but they can't speak or touch or feel things—like living ghosts, I guess," Fi finished matter-of-factly.

Jack's jaw dropped as he watched her dump some change into the coin slot of the phone and start to dial.

Frustrated, Jack continued. "Fi, what are you saying? That she was really in school at the time? Will you stop dialing and listen to me?"

Fi shook her head at Jack and motioned to him to be quiet. She said into the phone, "Hi, is Claire there?"

Someone on the other end said something.

"Sorry, wrong number." Fi bit her lip and felt

sheepish. "One down," she muttered, then began to dial another number.

"Are you saying she left her body at *school*? Nobody in their right mind would do that! Like why didn't she just cut class or something normal?"

Fi stopped dialing. With a frown she gazed directly at Jack. "Y'know, I never thought about that. Good question. Maybe she's not the type to cut class," Fi mused. "But leaving her body in a chem lab seems kind of scary. If she left her body in the wrong place and something happened to it . . ." Fi finished dialing the number. "Now I've *got* to find her."

"You can't just call people out of the blue and talk to them about astral projection, Fi. That's really too out there—even for you!"

"I just want to talk to her. One conversation will set the record straight here. Maybe you're right, Jack. Maybe I *am* barking up the wrong tree," Fi conceded, though inwardly she was sure she was on the right track. Nothing else but astral projection made sense. She *had* seen the girl in the yearbook at the carnival. And the girl did walk through her like Fi was made of thin air.

On the third ring a woman answered. "Hello?"

"You're off the deep end, Fi," Jack said. "I don't want to know you. This is too embarrassing." With a disapproving shake of his head, Jack wandered back toward Clu and the video games.

Watching Jack go, Fi relaxed a little. "Oh, hi! Ummm—is Claire there? I'm . . . a friend of hers."

The voice on the other end of the phone answered. "One moment please. She's upstairs studying."

"Great, she's home!" Fi murmured as she heard the woman put down the phone.

Fi leaned back against the phone booth and twiddled the cord. She stared up toward the front of the arcade. Jack had joined Clu at the pinball machine. The boys were intent on the game. Fi's gaze drifted past them as she waited for Claire to come to the phone.

Slanty sunlight was spilling in the front door of the game parlor. A figure stepped through the door. It was a tall, leggy girl, with enormous eyes and lovely red hair.

Fi's jaw dropped. *Claire Avner!* she realized in a flash. What is she doing here?

Claire moved gracefully into the game room, looking around. She turned in Fi's direction, her elegant eyebrows arched upward, and she flashed Fi a radiant smile.

Suddenly the receiver in Fi's hand buzzed with a woman's voice. "Claire? You have a phone call." Fi stared at the phone, then back up at Claire. She sneaked out! Fi thought. Now she's going to get into trouble.

"Claire?" The woman called again, this time sounding anxious. Fi continued to listen. She heard a sound as if someone were knocking on a door.

Fi looked up at Claire, wondering if she should warn her to get home. But even as Fi started to open her mouth, Claire's head turned quickly away from Fi. Her whole body seemed to grow tense, and she started back toward the door of the game room.

"Don't go!" Fi started to call after her, then heard the woman's voice on the phone, calling even more sharply.

"Claire? Are you in there? You have a call."

"Um—Mrs. Avner—" Fi started to say she'd call back later, when she saw Claire approach the front door, then shimmer in a shaft of sunlight and disappear.

Fi sank back against the phone booth, her

heart thumping like crazy. Again the girl had vanished into thin air, right before her eyes, but where—

"Hi." A girl's voice was on the other end of the phone. She sounded hesitant, shy, and sort of half asleep.

Fi's blood ran cold. She was afraid to ask, but she had to know. Had the girl she'd just seen in front of her in the arcade somehow materialized back home in the space of a heartbeat? "Is this Claire? Claire Avner?"

"Yes." The flat, emotionless voice on the phone didn't match the vibrant, confident girl Fi had just seen in the arcade.

"Who's this?" Claire's pale voice asked.

But Fi couldn't answer. Her heart seemed to stop. I am not going to faint! she told herself firmly, but dropped the phone receiver as if it were burning her hand.

"Jack—" she tried to call her brother, but her voice seemed to have deserted her.

Chapter Eight

"I'm telling you guys," Fi insisted later that afternoon. She, Clu, and Jack were strolling down a wide street lined with upscale suburban houses. "Claire was in the arcade, looking right at me. The next second, she dissolved into thin air. A second later a girl was talking to me on the phone, from Claire Avner's house, saying *she* was Claire." Fi stopped in her tracks and folded her arms across her chest. "Explain that, Jack!"

"Easy!" Jack scoffed. "The girl on the phone wasn't Claire. Or not the same Claire. Or whoever you saw in the arcade was a girl who looked like her." He kicked at a pile of leaves on the sidewalk.

He looked up at Fi, and shook his head slowly. "This is all so crazy." At Fi's insistence Jack, Clu, and Fi were on their way to find Claire Avner's house. "You act as if there's no other possible explanation than some girl is abandoning her body to float around an arcade. Sis, this makes no sense!"

"And how come we didn't see her?" Clu asked, shoving his hands in the pockets of the light windbreaker he'd picked up back at the tour bus. "We were right there."

"Because you goofballs were too busy with your video game," Fi countered quickly.

"And say you're right," Clu continued. "Why wouldn't she just go to the arcade after school? I mean, why leave your body home and let your spirit, or soul or ghost or whatever it is, hang out at an arcade?"

"Good question." Jack nodded, thumping Clu on the shoulder.

"Makes me wonder, too," Fi mused, as they strolled down the street. The Avners' neighborhood was near the Bardo Hotel and not far from the carnival grounds. "But I don't care if you believe me or not," Fi added, stopping at a corner and looking up at a street sign. "This is her block, and in a few minutes we'll find out what's going on."

"Yeah, like some girl is going to let three strangers into her house and discuss the finer points of astral projection with them." Jack heaved a big sigh, but continued down the street after Fi.

As she continued down the block, Fi checked out the mailboxes. "Hey, this is it!" she exclaimed, pointing to a mailbox at the end of a longish blacktop driveway. Fi craned her neck to see beyond the evergreen bushes flanking the drive. A modern ranch-style house greeted her eyes. To the left of some lower shrubs, a neatly painted sign said THE AVNERS. A flagstone walk led from the sign to the front steps of the house.

"Awesome joint!" Clu remarked, taking in the landscaping. "It's like someone ironed the lawn, man!"

"Starched the bushes!" Jack chuckled.

Fi put her hand to her mouth and stifled a nervous giggle. The boys were right. The place looked so formal, the whole idea of knocking on the front door was beginning to feel a little scary.

"Maybe you guys should stay out of sight," Fi suggested, dropping her voice to a conspiratorial whisper. "She might totally freak out to find us all on her doorstep." That is, if Claire answered the door. If her mom or dad did, Fi would just die. What in the world would she say?

Jack tapped her shoulder, and motioned toward a clump of bushes nearby. "Would you hurry up already, and don't act too weird around these people. Folks who live in a place like this aren't likely to take too kindly to your astral projection theory, sis."

"Yeah they might think you're some kind of con artist," Clu added, looking nervous.

Jack shrugged. "Whatever, Fi—bailing you out of jail will cost me my allowance until I'm like fifty." Jack tugged at Clu's sleeve, and the two boys ducked behind the shrubs.

Fi waited a moment, inhaled deeply, then walked right up to the door. She rang the bell, and waited for what seemed like forever. She heard footsteps.

The door cracked open, and Claire peeked out. Fi stared at the girl in disbelief. The girl on the doorstep matched Claire Avner's yearbook photo: she was plain, with pale skin and a tired, sad expression on her pretty features. She looked lifeless, and except for the clothes she was wearing she barely resembled the girl at the carnival. She also looked strangely transparent. As if she wasn't quite all there.

At the sight of Fi a shock of recognition fleetingly crossed her face. And Fi knew instantly her hunch had been right. Claire Avner—or at least her spirit—*had* seen Fi before, at the carnival and the arcade. Before Fi could say anything, Claire's expression shifted to wariness. Narrowing her large green eyes, she tucked her long, slim hands into the pockets of her snug jeans and regarded Fi coolly. "Can I help you?"

"Well . . . can I help *you?*" Fi replied nervously. "Do you recognize me?"

Claire arched her eyebrow, but didn't answer.

"The carnival? The arcade?" Fi prodded, holding her gaze. Claire dropped her eyes and kicked at a crack in the cement step.

"I don't know what you're talking about," she murmured, and began closing the door in Fi's face.

Fi put her hand on the doorframe, stopping her, just as the crunch of gravel sounded in the driveway.

Both girls turned as a shiny black BMW rolled smoothly toward the garage. Fi looked quickly from the car back to Claire. Claire's face had turned a whiter shade of pale.

A tall auburn-haired man got out, carrying a briefcase and wearing a well-cut suit. He flicked a remote alarm control at the car, and started toward the front walk.

"Your dad?" Fi asked.

Claire visibly gulped.

Fi plunged on. "Does he know what you're up to?"

Claire flashed Fi a panicky look. "I don't know you, why don't you just leave me alone?" she said. "Why are you bothering me, anyway?"

"I saw you at the carnival and I talked to you. I know what you're doing. And I want to help," Fi pleaded.

Claire shot a quick glance in her father's direction. He had detoured to the mailbox to pick up the mail. "Please, leave me alone!"

"No," Fi insisted. "You need help."

"I don't need help!" Claire whispered sharply. "I'm perfectly fine." But she opened the door wide enough for Fi to come inside. Fi hesitated on the threshold. She reached out a finger and touched Claire's shoulder.

Claire recoiled. "What'd you do that for?"

"I'm sorry. I was just checking that you are really you—in the flesh."

Claire bit her lip, but didn't volunteer any information as she ushered Fi into the house. Fi's eyes widened as she stepped into the foyer. The ceilings were high for a one-story house, and light flooded through a skylight, illuminating a modern geometric painting hanging on one wall.

Hoping she'd gotten all the bubble gum off her sneakers, Fi cautiously stepped on the creamy white carpet. The foyer opened into a large family room, with a formal dining area at one end. Through the arched opening of one wall, Fi could see an ultramodern kitchen. Chrome appliances gleamed on the countertops. The place looked positively sterilized.

The living room furniture was upholstered in various shades of cream and white, and the bleached wood floors looked clean enough for a person to eat off of.

People live this way? Fi was flabbergasted. The Avners' home looked like a museum. It belonged on a different planet than Fi's comfortably cluttered old Victorian house back in Hope Springs.

"So what do you want?" Claire's weak voice brought Fi back to the present. Claire guided Fi down a short hallway that seemed to lead to the back of the house.

Fi swept her bangs out of her eyes and said earnestly. "Claire, I know what you're up to. This out-of-body stuff."

"Shhh!" Claire warned, just as the front door opened and quickly closed. Fi looked past Claire's shoulder to see her father standing in the doorway, holding an open letter in his hand. He put down his briefcase next to the glass-topped foyer table.

He glanced over Claire's shoulder and spotted Fi.

"Dad," Claire said quickly. "Uh . . . this is . . ."

"Fi Phillips." Fi poked out her hand. "Nice to meet you, Mr. Avner."

"One of Claire's friends?" Mr. Avner asked, but didn't give Fi a chance to answer. "Claire, we have to talk," he said. He hesitated and looked at Fi again, then motioned for Claire to step a little aside.

Claire followed him into the family room, and stood at the door, staring down at her feet, a sullen expression on her face. Her father lowered his voice but Fi could hear every word he said.

"Claire, can you explain why I got a call from your guidance counselor today?"

"Dad—" Claire gasped.

"What's this about a guidance counselor?"

Fi turned at the sound of a woman's voice. *Must be Claire's mother!* It didn't take a brain surgeon to figure that out. The tall forty-something woman was a sophisticated, elegantly dressed version of her daughter: the same fair coloring, reddish hair, and enormous eyes. Her makeup was perfect, and she looked stunning in a pale green dinner suit.

"Claire's been falling asleep in class. Her teachers are getting worried . . ."

Catching sight of Fi, Mrs. Avner put a warning hand up and stopped her husband from saying more. She shot Fi a questioning look.

Fi hazarded a small, sheepish smile. She shifted from foot to foot, feeling awkward.

"We'll talk about this later," Mrs. Avner said quickly, glancing at her watch. "We've got a business dinner meeting. But we'll be back around nine or so. Supper's in the fridge, ready to heat up." She touched Claire's cheek. "If there's a problem we can stay home and—"

"There's no problem, Mom. Really," Claire insisted. "Go out, okay? Don't change your plans."

Mrs. Avner studied Claire a moment, then with an uncertain smile, said good-bye and followed her husband out the door.

Through the living room window, Fi watched Claire's parents climb into the car. A wave of sympathy for Claire washed over Fi. At the slightest whiff that her kids might be in some kind of trouble, Molly would cancel dinner in a heartbeat to spend time with them and ferret the problem out.

"So now, what's this help you think I need?" Claire inquired, walking up to Fi. Beneath her sullen tone, Fi detected a note of fear.

Fi replied with a question of her own. "How'd you get into this stuff?"

Claire shrugged, then pointed down the hall. "Let's talk in my room," she suggested.

Fi followed Claire down the short hallway to the back of the house. Claire opened the door to her room. Like the rest of the house it was spotless and somehow uninviting. Fi couldn't imagine enjoying being in this room, studying there, or chatting to friends on her computer. Everything was too pastel, too perfect, too cold.

The bedroom looked out on a sprawling back-yard, the lawn butting up against a thickly wooded area.

Careful to move a pale pink teddy bear out of her way, Claire sat down cross-legged on her bed, while Fi slipped off her blue knapsack and put it carefully beside Claire's desk. She sat gingerly on the edge of a white wicker chair.

Claire regarded Fi a moment. "I don't *want* to talk about this."

"We have to, believe me," Fi insisted.

"I've never talked to anyone about—about what happens to me if I let it—"

"Does it have to do with your parents? Do you do it to get away from all this?" Fi waved her hands around the room.

"No—nothing like that—not exactly." Claire flopped down on the bed, folding her arms under her head. She got a dreamy expression on her face, and for a long moment said nothing.

Fi forced herself to be patient. Finally Claire sat up again. She propped her chin on her hands and began to speak. At first her voice was expressionless, but as she told her story, her eyes began to shine, and her whole face and body seemed to come to life.

"When I was little, I used to go to this tree house, in the woods out back. My parents don't know about it—some kids must have built it ages ago. I discovered it when I was about seven. I used to spend hours there. Just to get away."

"So you do want to escape . . ." Fi interjected.

"Sort of. It's just they expect so much of me. I *am* smart. I'm good at school, and I used to love it—being a brain. My folks got me all these tutors, and I've had more private lessons—in everything from French to tennis—than anyone could possibly want. All I hear from my folks is that if I work hard enough I can be anything I want." Claire pressed her hands to her temples. "The problem is, I don't want what they want. I just want to have fun." She looked quickly up at Fi.

Fi nodded. "Why not?" she commented cautiously.

"Because when you're working so hard, even at playing tennis, there's no time for fun. So that's when it started happening. One day I tuned out my math tutor, and found that I could sort of drift right out of my body, and head somewhere else . . . at first, another part of the house. Later I figured out I could go clear across town if I wanted to."

"What's it feel like?" Fi asked, leaning forward in her chair. As worried as she was about Claire, she was madly curious.

"You can't imagine," Claire exclaimed animatedly. "It's like—I can be anyone. I can look different. I feel so free!" She spread her arms in an expansive gesture, and for a moment Fi glimpsed the strong confident girl she'd seen at the carnival.

"Sounds great, Claire, but while you're off being whoever you want, what happens to your body?" Fi questioned cautiously.

"What do you mean?"

"Like today you left it at school to go to a carnival."

Claire giggled softly. "Yeah. In the chem lab." She smiled down at her hands. Glancing up at Fi again, she shrugged. "What of it?"

"Someone might notice. Something might happen to you."

Claire smiled a tolerant smile. "I've been doing this for ages. Nothing's happened to me."

"Yet," Fi stated firmly. "Where else have you left your body, besides school or home?"

"Now that you ask," Claire admitted, sounding a bit uncomfortable, "I did fall asleep a couple of times in some weird places. When I didn't mean to."

"Weird places, like . . ." Fi urged her to go on.

"Like at the bus stop once. But somebody always wakes me up!"

"I'm not sure that's the point," Fi mused. "It's more like what if they can't wake you up. Or what if something happens to your body when you're not in it!"

"Hey, don't get so heavy about this!" Claire admonished. "It's fun, it's free, and I don't hurt anyone. Besides, it sure beats my everyday study, study, study sort of life."

"Makes sense," Fi admitted. "But it's still a pretty dangerous thing to do." Fi jumped up and reached for her backpack. "Before I came over here I went back to my mom's tour bus and picked up some stuff." Unzipping one of the compartments in her pack, Fi pulled out a bunch of papers.

"This stuff you're doing—it's called astral projection," Fi said, ruffling through the papers looking for what she'd downloaded the night before. "Look, I know it seems harmless to you, but dangerous stuff can happen if you go too far with it. Like, have you ever heard of the Monroe-Tart OBE experiments? They did 'em at the University of California in 1965. See, there was this Virginia businessman, Robert Monroe, who left his body all the time, and what they found was that after a while he started to have problems reentering his body; like one time, he even entered a corpse—by mistake. Here, you can keep this stuff, and read it and . . ." Fi went to hand the papers to Claire.

She gasped. Claire was asleep on the bed. Rather *one* Claire was on the bed.

The second Claire had her back toward Fi. As Fi watched, Claire's astral self walked up to her bedroom wall, and pressing out her hands, walked right through it.

"Claire—don't!" Fi cried, rushing to the window and flinging it open. Claire was already halfway across the lawn, heading toward the woods.

"Claire!" Fi called again.

At the sound of Fi's voice, Claire glanced back over her shoulder and threw Fi a twisted smile.

Chapter Nine

Halfway through Fi's lecture on astral projection, Claire glared at her from the bed. *Oh, just chill out!* Claire commanded silently, flopping down and burying her face under her pillow.

Claire hated being lectured—about *anything*. She got more than her fair dose of talking-tos from her parents for not being the absolutely perfect straight-A student, and from her teachers lately for falling asleep in class. Now from this perfect stranger who had somehow stumbled on Claire's sacred private world, and was threatening to ruin it with all her dire predictions of who knew what.

Getting lost in space or something. Waking up inside a corpse. Claire did not have to listen to this. Stretching out on her back, Claire closed her eyes and crossed her hands over her chest. She took one deep breath after another, like she'd seen on some TV yoga show. She imagined she were floating, like a feather, a dandelion puff, a cloud. By the time she drew her fifth breath, Claire was standing outside her body, looking down at herself—asleep. What a loser, she thought, looking at her pale, thin self. She immediately pictured how she wanted to look and could feel her shoulders straighten, and warmth rush to her cheeks. When she ran her fingers through her auburn waves, her hair felt fluffy and bouncy.

She faced the mirror over her dresser—she could see Fi still rummaging through papers by the desk. She could see her room, the slanty afternoon light spilling through the open curtains. But of course she couldn't see herself. She *knew* that in her astral body she looked incredible, she had heard guys—guys like Clu and Jack—say so but she had never *seen* her astral self in a mirror. To mirrors she was invisible.

With a deep sigh, Claire cast one last look at Fi, then braced herself for the shock of walking through the shuttered windows. She pushed against the white painted slats and her body shuddered with the familiar, deeply disturbing jolt. *As if all my molecules are being jangled*, she thought, emerging in the backyard behind her bedroom wall.

It was the worst part of leaving her body— almost.

Lately the terrifying part was getting back *into*

her body. As if every time she floated off from her body, it shrank a little. She often felt like she barely fit into it anymore.

Stop thinking that way! Claire scolded herself as she headed past the flower garden toward the woods. She fluffed out her hair, straightened her back, and lengthened her stride. It was Fi's fault she was suddenly spooked. What did Fi know about astral projecting, anyway? Just some garbage she'd downloaded from the Internet.

Claire cast one last look back toward the house. Fi was calling to her from the deck. Claire shot her a tight smile.

Stifling a pang of regret, Claire continued toward the woods. Too bad about Fi. Part of her wished she could really explain to someone how great it was to leave your body. But Fi seemed tuned in to only the bad parts of astral projection. And Claire was not in the mood to hear about the bad parts. Life outside her body was so much more fun than being her ordinary self that Claire was willing to risk all sorts of dangers.

When she reached the trees, she paused. A narrow trail led through the brush, then forked. One path wound toward the outskirts of town and the fairgrounds. The other ran straight back toward Main Street, in the direction of school and The Game Charade. A breeze rustled the branches over Claire's head and lifted her hair off her face. Shading her eyes from the sun, Claire made her decision. Hooking her fingers in the belt loops of her jeans, she made for the fairgrounds and tonight's country music festival.

Her parents *never* let her go to pop music concerts. Now was her chance. And maybe she'd run into those two guys again—Fi's friends. Hadn't they mentioned something about being into music, and one of their dads being a roadie?

Letter by letter the neon sign above the Bardo Hotel's Badlands dance club lit up, flashed three times, then went dark again. The flickering light spilled through the tinted window of the tour bus into the dimly lit common area. Fi had her Walkman turned on low, tuned into an all-night rock oldies station, but her attention was half focused on the screen of her laptop.

Half of Fi's mind was still back with Claire that afternoon in Claire's room. "Man, did I blow it!" she grumbled now.

She could hear the TV in Clu and Jack's room, tuned in to a loud late-night talk show. Fi glanced at the clock on the bottom of her computer screen—her mom's gig should be over soon.

"Hey!" Jack said, coming from the back of the bus. He was dressed in dark gray sweats, with the Molly Phillips Band logo printed across the shirt. His dark hair was damp, his cheeks were pink from the shower, and he had a towel draped around his neck. He propped his hip on the back of the couch and lifted one earphone of Fi's Walkman.

Fi looked up. "Hey!" she said, happy to see him.

Jack brandished a bag of microwave popcorn at Fi.

She nodded eagerly, and tossed her headset on the table. Leaning back against the wall of the bus, she fingered the hem of her flannel pajamas.

"Clu conked out in front of the tube," Jack said, putting the bag of popcorn in the microwave and punching the Start button. He plunked himself down on the gray-cushioned window seat next to Fi. "I've been thinking about that girl. . . ."

"Me, too!" Fi grimaced. "Probably pretty different thoughts!" she teased.

Jack thumped his heart. "Can't help it, little sister. The girl's got me. I can't get her out of my mind." In spite of his clowning around, Jack sounded defensive.

"Jack, I know you like her. I think she might be a pretty nice person—in *person*," Fi stressed, "but she's in trouble, Jack and . . ." Fi threw up her hands in frustration. "Why am I sometimes such a total *dweeb?* I tried to help her. But what did I do?" Fi jumped up and crossed the narrow room. "I made things worse. I turned her off. More like scared her off."

"How?" Jack wondered, tossing his towel on the back of a chair.

"Instead of just trying to *talk* to her, like girl to girl, I started pulling out all these papers I printed out yesterday: reports from E.S.P. and astral projection conferences, and blabbing about all these technical details and studies—everything I downloaded from the Web!"

"I see you're still at it!" Jack pointed at the laptop screen. "What's all that stuff, anyway?"

"The astral projection news group." Fi shrugged. "I can't help it, Jack. I need to know more. Right now I need more ammunition to convince Claire she's headed for trouble."

The microwave pinged and Fi emptied the bag of popcorn into a glass bowl. She offered it to Jack.

He dug in and jerked his head in the direction of the screen. "Y'know, people on the Internet have too much time on their hands. Who are these people who spend half the night talking about floating out of their bodies?"

"People like me, I guess," Fi admitted, hunkering down on a cushion across from Jack. Putting the popcorn bowl between them, she continued, "Unfortunately *not* kids like Claire. She's pretty clueless about what might happen to her if she keeps leaving her body. I just wanted to reach out to her. The girl needs help."

"Hate to disappoint you, Fi, but I still don't buy this out-of-body stuff," Jack admitted. "But say you're right—which is impossible here—why is it all such a problem?"

"Because she keeps leaving her body to escape from her life. Even when she was a kid she used to escape from her parents into this tree house in the woods behind her house," Fi confided. "Problem is, you can't get in much trouble in a tree house, but escaping from her body—man, that's a whole other thing!"

"What's she got to escape from?" Jack sounded skeptical. "Her life didn't look *that* miserable to me. That was some house she's got, Fi. The kid's not hurting for money." Jack lifted his shoulders in a shrug. "Her parents looked pretty okay. You were inside, but when they went to the car they were laughing like two ordinary people heading out to dinner."

"Exactly!" Fi said. "They know something's wrong with their kid, but they still head off to dinner as if Claire and her problems are something they can take care of later. Mom wouldn't do that."

"No. She wouldn't, but she's Mom." Jack scarfed down the last of the popcorn, and stood up. "Different families have different styles."

Fi shook her head adamantly. "Whatever, that girl's headed for trouble, and she needs help. She's got to talk to her parents—or something."

Jack shook his head. "Look, I'm not exactly sure what's going on with this girl . . . though I *am* pretty sure it's not what *you* think is going on, but how about we all try looking for her one more time tomorrow? People trust you with their problems Fi, even I've noticed that!" he admitted, laughing. "Maybe if you hear her out first, without bombarding her with all this techno-speak, she'll get the message."

Jack reassured Fi with a pat on the back, then stood up.

"Hey, thanks for that Jack . . . I think," Fi said. Was that, like, a compliment? Fi marveled, as the door to the bus opened and Molly stepped inside.

She was wearing Dad's old suede jacket over a long black velvet antique dress—the new stage outfit she'd picked up that afternoon. Her color was high and her eyes were bright as she jangled the keys to her hotel room in one hand.

"Hey, guys. Come to tuck you in," she announced, walking farther into the common area. "You sure you kids are okay sleeping in here on your own tonight?" Fi and Jack exchanged an exasperated glance. Usually during their gigs, all of them slept in a motel. But with the carnival in town, most of the rooms were booked, and Molly had relaxed her rule letting the kids stay alone in the bus at night, for once.

"We're fine, Mom, really," Fi said, tossing the last kernel of popcorn at her mother.

Molly laughed an easy, comfortable laugh, and Fi couldn't believe how happy her mom looked. Being on the road again, performing, even at these tiny hole-in-the-wall clubs, was bringing her to life again. Audience reaction was like a transfusion or something.

Jack sat down in the window seat and patted a cushion next to him. "How'd the show go?"

"The place was packed—in spite of that country music thing at the carnival. Wasn't an empty seat in the house," Molly said proudly. "And both sets went really well. Even the last one. This hot guy up front kept wanting to jam with us."

"No way!" Fi exclaimed, drawing up her knees. "What'd you do?"

With a low throaty laugh, Molly said wickedly, "I hammered a low E power chord and blew him off the stage with my new subwoofers."

"Get outta here, Mom!" Jack guffawed as Fi winced and put her hands over her ears.

"He must have died!"

"Not quite," Molly said truthfully. "But I doubt he'll pull that one again on the next band that comes through here."

"Well, they can't say your music doesn't move people." Jack yawned. "I'm heading to bed. G'night." Jack rumpled Fi's hair, then stood up and kissed his mom.

"Good night, sweetheart," she said, as he grabbed his towel and headed back toward his room. A second later the sound on the TV went off.

Molly stretched her legs on the window seat and quietly regarded Fi. "What's up, baby?" she asked. "Everything okay?"

Fi hesitated. Should she mention Claire and her problems to her mom? Or more like *could* she? Molly was almost as skeptical as Jack about Fi's interest in weird stuff. Fi knew her mother worried about her passion for the supernatural. Even though sometimes Fi felt that Molly kind of believed in ghosts herself—or at least her dad's ghost.

Fi forced a smile and finally answered. "Yeah . . ."

"Really?" Molly reached out and tenderly brushed Fi's bangs out of her eyes.

"Really," Fi answered, fingering the fringe on Molly's jacket and avoiding her mother's eyes.

"Fiona," Molly said, slowly getting up, "you'd tell me if you needed help with something, right?"

Fi thought a moment, then made a decision. If things didn't work out with Claire tomorrow, she would tell Molly. Exactly what she would tell her, Fi had no idea. With a clear conscience she said, "Yeah, I would."

Chapter Ten

The next afternoon at the carnival, Fi stood near the Tilt-A-Whirl, perplexed. A sharp wind whipped down the fairway, and seemed to scurry down Fi's neck, beneath her sweatshirt. She tightened the drawstring and shivered. "She's got to be here, but I don't even know where to start looking," Fi remarked with a deep sigh.

"What makes you think Claire's gonna be here?" Jack inquired, jamming his fists in the pockets of his jeans.

"Man, if I were her, I'd head back to that arcade, the one we checked out yesterday. It's not the arctic zone there, dudes!" Clu hopped from foot to foot, blowing on his hands. In spite of the bright sun, an early taste of high-country winter was in the air.

"I can't swear she's here," Fi admitted. "When I called her house, her mom said she hadn't come home from school yet. She sounded worried. She said when I found Claire, to tell her to call home." Fi hesitated.

"Like she'll listen to you on that one," Jack remarked, looking around the fairgrounds.

Fi followed his glance. The crowd was thicker today, maybe because it was a Friday afternoon. It seemed half of Bardo High was jostling to scope out the rides.

"Anyway, I've just got a hunch this is where she'll come. The carnival's closing tomorrow. If she wants to take in the scene here, she's only got a couple of days. She can check out the arcade anytime," Fi concluded, continuing to search the crowd.

"Bingo!" Clu's exclamation made Fi turn around. "Is that a vision I see before me, or what?" Clu pointed through a break in the crowd, toward the turnstiles.

Dressed in a neatly pressed blue work shirt that hung out over her jeans, Claire was emerging from the woods beyond the carnival grounds. Without stopping at the ticket booth, she swung through the turnstile. The ticket taker didn't seem to notice she hadn't paid admission.

"All right, Clu!" Fi thumped him on the back, then, making a megaphone of her hands, shouted over the din of the barkers and music. "Hey, Claire! Over here!" She waved vigorously in Claire's direction, but the crowd closed in around her. Fi stood on tiptoe trying to glimpse Claire's auburn hair.

"Lost her!" she grumbled, as a gust of wind whipped her long hair across her face. Annoyed, she pushed it back and secured it with a blue barrette.

"Maybe not—follow that blue shirt!" Clu urged, darting off through the crowd.

Jack bolted after him. Fi followed, but then the girl stopped at a vendor. Getting a good glimpse of her face, Fi groaned. "Wrong girl!"

Clu stopped in front of a hot dog stand and shook his head in dismay. "I coulda sworn that was Claire."

"It wasn't, but isn't that her now?" Jake started off in the opposite direction. This time the girl they trailed looked back over her shoulder. No doubt now. It was Claire. She taunted them with a smile.

Fi waved, and called out, frustrated. "Claire, wait up!" Fi elbowed her way through the throng. But before she could get within ten feet of Claire, the girl ducked down a narrow alley between some tents.

"She's doing this on purpose!" Clu exclaimed. "She wants to lose us."

"Or play games," Jack said, beginning to sound annoyed.

"Look, you guys," Fi suggested. "Go cut her off on the other side of these tents. I'll circle this way. We're bound to run into her."

While Clu and Jack headed to the left of the big striped tent, Fi went to the right. She raced clear around the circular structure and slammed right into Jack.

"Whoa!" Jack caught her by her arms.

"Where'd she go?" Clu gasped, looking past Fi.

"Not in that direction," Fi replied, rubbing her arms.

Jack frowned. "This girl is definitely messing with us."

Fi fought to catch her breath. "She must have already left her body. We were chasing her astral form. That's the only explanation."

"You mean *your* only explanation. Get real, Fi," Jack grumbled.

Fi was in no mood to argue. "Look," she said sharply, "you believe she has a body, right?"

Jack and Clu shoved each other and chuckled. "Yeah!" they both drawled, almost in unison. "You could say that!" Clu added, with a goofy grin.

Fi gritted her teeth. "Good. You guys go find

it. I'll look for the part you *don't* believe in," she shot pointedly at Jack.

With an angry toss of her head, Fi blew out her breath, and turned abruptly on her heel. She gasped. Claire was standing directly across a narrow alley heading into Mr. Spooky's House of Glass.

Fi was about to start directly toward the tent, but some instinct prompted her to hide. Darting behind a cotton candy stand, she peered around the corner of the booth. Claire was still outside the entrance to the wood and glass construction labeled MR. SPOOKY'S. She looked first to her right, then her left. Fi was almost sure Claire looked disappointed that for once she wasn't being followed.

After a second, Claire ducked into Mr. Spooky's. Fi crept quietly around the other side. This time she'd sneak up on Claire, before she had a chance to bolt—and maybe before she totally disappeared.

"We should have stayed at the fairground, dude!" Clu grumbled as he and Jack maneuvered their way through the forest.

Faint carnival sounds wafted from the fairgrounds. "The carnival, even without Claire, is more fun than this wilderness."

"What wilderness?" Jack scoffed, pushing through a clump of stubborn, red-leaved bushes. "Besides, this is a shortcut to her house. It's just through those woods. She probably ditched us and headed for home. C'mon, man, get a move on."

"Well, sorry, old pal," Clu grumbled, as the boys emerged into the thinner underbrush of the forest. "I never signed on to be a Boy Scout!"

"Me neither, and if you want to bail out, that's fine with me," Jack declared. "Less competition."

"Hey, you won't lose me that easily," Clu protested, then yelped. "Ow! Something *else* just bit me! And y'know, that green stuff over there is probably poison ivy, or deadly nightshade, or something!"

"That's not poison ivy, and we'd get back to her house sooner if you'd let your feet do the running instead of your mouth," Jack told him.

Suddenly a loud crack sounded right over their head. Clu gripped Jack's arm. "Man, what's that? A bear or—"

"Shhhh!" Jack silenced him. He pointed up. "The sound came from up there."

"I know *that*. The tree is falling—there's probably some very large animal about to—"

"Quiet! But something *is* up there. And it's not an animal." Jack craned his neck. "Hey, Clu. Didn't Fi say something about Claire having a tree house in the woods?"

"Did she?"

"Doesn't matter—that's a tree house," Jack declared, shading his eyes to get a better look. "Bet ya ten-to-one it's hers."

"More like 'used to be hers,'" said Clu, stepping back to get a better look. "That heap of junk sure looks like it's seen better days."

"And more than its share of storms," Jack added. "It looks awfully rickety."

"So does the ladder," Clu stated, testing the weathered rungs running up the side of the thick tree trunk. The boards were fixed to the tree with rusty nails and rattled slightly as he tugged at them. Clu glanced up. "Hey, wasn't she wearing something blue?"

"Yeah, a work shirt," Jack said, following Clu's glance. He spotted a familiar sky-blue shirt. "Someone's up there."

"Not just someone. Claire," Clu said. "But how'd she get up there so fast? We left the carnival maybe five minutes after we last saw her. Is she some kind of long-distance runner?"

"Beats me," Jack said, as he started to climb the ladder. "But I bet it's her."

As he reached the top of the ladder, Jack looked through a little window cut in the side of the tree house. Claire was lying on her side, on top of an old ratty mat. One hand was flung over her head, the other wrapped around her waist. As Jack watched she didn't even seem to be breathing. A wave of fear swept over Jack—was she alive? Finally, she drew one small, very shallow breath, then, after a long interval, another.

Jack relaxed, just a little. "I don't believe this," he turned and whispered loudly to Clu. "It really is Claire, and she's sound asleep!"

Chapter Eleven

Fi counted to ten, then followed Claire into Mr. Spooky's House of Glass. Stepping inside, she was dazzled by the light. Every surface was made of glass: window glass, mirror glass, funky distorted bubbly glass. Every piece of glass shone bright as diamonds.

As soon as she entered, Fi was faced with a dozen reflections of herself. All those Fi's staring back at her made her dizzy, confused, and a little self-conscious. She tugged down her shirt, smoothed her hair, and made a resolution to trim her bangs—tonight!

"Welcome to our mirror maze," the ticket taker said. Fi looked to her right. A silver-haired woman with a very young face and silver rings on every finger was seated at a card table. Wearing a flowing tribal-print dress, she looked like a fortune-teller.

"This is a maze?" Fi asked, digging in her pocket for her admission ticket.

The woman punched her ticket and nodded. "The whole point is to find your way out."

Fi swallowed hard. "Ummm—did you see which way my friend went?"

"Your friend?" The woman repeated, a puzzled expression crossing her face. "No one's been here for hours, dearie."

Fi cocked her head in disbelief, then she remembered. Astral bodies were invisible in mirrors. "Right. The mirrors. Of course." She flashed the ticket taker an apologetic grin. "Sorry. My mistake," she said, trying to ignore the knot in her stomach.

How would she ever find Claire in this place? she wondered, carefully feeling her way down the start of the maze. She hadn't gone five steps when she walked right into a wall of glass. She felt with her hands, and found another opening to the left.

She turned, and there, at the end of the same corridor was Claire, separated by several walls of glass.

"Claire!" Fi hurried forward and stepped right into a glass partition. Claire seemed to hear her; she gazed over her shoulder and smiled at Fi. Then she passed right through the glass. Fi tried to follow her, but even keeping her in sight, she had to feel her way.

Everywhere she turned she saw reflections of

herself. It was like seeing her own echo or something. She hurried, her footsteps ringing out against the floor.

Sometimes Claire was in front of her, sometimes to her left or right. But wherever she walked, her footsteps were silent.

"Hey, Claire," Fi called out after a few minutes, "all this cat-and-mouse stuff is okay, but I wish you'd stop. I'd like to talk to you."

Claire paused. She studied Fi a moment, then shrugged. Fi approached her cautiously, afraid to scare her away. "I was thinking about what you said. About how cool it is to leave your body. I have to admit . . . I wish I could try it myself."

Claire bit her lip. She nodded at Fi. She opened her mouth as if to say something, but no words came out. For a moment Claire looked frustrated.

Fi stepped closer to her. Jack had told her to listen to Claire, but how could she listen to this astral projection who didn't have the power to speak? It was all up to Fi, and she chose her words carefully. "But I'm still worried about you. I mean, even if the dangerous stuff never happens to you there are still some things you can only do when you're in your body." Fi paused. "Like talk to a friend?"

Claire nodded vigorously.

Encouraged, Fi went on. "Look, I know you've got enough people telling you what to do. You don't need me on top of it. All I want to say is that you're obviously an amazing person, and I think it would be sad if you never gave your folks a chance to know who you *really* are. If you told them what's wrong—that you need some space, I bet they would listen. Have you tried?"

Claire looked down at her feet, and kicked at the floor. Slowly, without looking up, she shook her head.

"Claire, look at me," Fi said, stepping closer. Claire surprised her by stepping through the glass wall that separated them and standing right in front of her. Fi pointed to a mirror across the wall. It was a funhouse kind of mirror. Fi looked about forty feet tall and one inch wide. Claire wasn't reflected in the mirror at all.

"See," Fi said, trying to lighten up. "It's no fun in your astral body. Like, how can you shop for clothes, or check out your hair? I bet you have no idea how incredible you look right now."

Claire put her hand to her lips, stifling a silent laugh.

In a more serious tone, Fi continued, "It's not real this way. Nothing's real. Not even you."

As Fi watched, Claire's expression shifted from curious to sad. Fi added quickly, "And maybe we could be friends. I might be back some time. Mom's got a gig in Jackson Hole this winter. That's not far from Bardo. Maybe we could go skiing or snowboarding. Of course, you'd have to travel in something normal like a car or bus to meet me."

Claire's face brightened, and she nodded eagerly.

Fi added with a laugh. "But you'll need your real body, and real legs for that."

Claire considered Fi carefully, then smiled a shy smile. She lifted her hand and tried to hit Fi a high five, but Fi's hand pushed right through Claire's and hit a glass wall.

"Ouch!" Fi exclaimed, while Claire looked horrified. "I'm okay," Fi assured her, then started to laugh heartily, until Claire slowly, silently joined in.

"I don't like this one bit!" Clu admitted as he and Jack stood inside the small tree house. Taller than Jack, Clu had to stoop to fit inside. The floorboards were creaky; half of them seemed to be missing.

Jack was staring down at Claire. "Is she asleep or what?" he remarked to Clu.

"With all this noise, she should wake up," Clu said, squinting at Claire. He stepped forward and the floor groaned beneath his feet. "Whoa. *Not* the smartest place to leave your body."

"You're getting as bad as Fi, Clu," Jack said impatiently. He looked at the sleeping girl and hazarded a smile. "All right, Claire. Enough with playing possum. We need to talk."

"She's not answering, dude," Clu pointed out.

"Like I didn't notice." Jack raised his voice and addressed Claire again. "We need to talk." She lay still as a log. "Hey, Claire. Claire!"

"I don't think she's faking it, Jack. I think she's out. Totally zonked."

"Dead to the world. I don't get it," Jack said, slowly making his way across the floor toward her. He stopped in front of her sleeping figure. "Claire?" he called again, this time louder.

Finally he leaned over to touch her shoulder. As he shifted his weight, the floorboards shuddered and creaked.

"Watch it!" Clu shouted too late. The tree house slowly began to sway.

SNAP! The sound was huge, explosive, and

suddenly the floor gave way beneath Claire and Jack. Jack grabbed Claire's leg as they both fell through the hole in the floor.

"Whoa, man!" Clu yelled, his hand shooting out to grab Jack's ankle.

"Got ya, man!" he cried. "Hang on to her!"

Jack dangled upside down half out of the tree house, twenty feet or more above the ground. "Pull me up!" he cried.

"I'm trying, man. I'm trying," Clu yelled back.

Jack shouted in a panicky voice, "She's like a dead weight. I don't know how long I can hold on to her."

"Why doesn't she wake up?" Clu cried, tightening his grip on Jack.

Jack tried to work his other hand down toward Claire's leg to hold on to her better. He stretched but couldn't reach. He needed her help. What was wrong with her, anyway?

"Wake up, Claire!" he shouted. "WAKE UP!"

Chapter Twelve

"I can't believe this!" Fi gasped between bouts of giggles. "I can't believe I tried to high-five an astral body!"

Tears of laughter streamed down Claire's face. She caught her breath and longed to tell Fi how silly she felt—silly, and dumb, and happier than she had been in ages. "Fi," she started to say, but of course no voice came out. She threw her hands up, and started to laugh again, when all at once she felt like someone kicked her in the stomach. She doubled over, clutching her middle.

"Claire?" Fi sounded alarmed.

Claire forced herself to stand up straight. She sought Fi's eyes. What's happening to me? she screamed. But Fi just kept staring at her.

Suddenly she felt as if someone had yanked her by the hair and was pulling her backward. She fought to stay put with Fi, where she felt safe. She stretched out her arms to Fi.

Fi reached for her, but Fi's fingers passed right through Claire's outstretched hands.

"Claire, what's happening? Where are you going? Claire!" Fi looked petrified.

Claire tried to keep focused on Fi, but felt herself whooshed backward, through the panes of glass, the mirrors, clear out of Mr. Spooky's House of Glass, and onto the fairway. Faster and faster, as if she were on ultra-high-speed rewind, she was pulled back at a sickening pace through space.

She zoomed at warp speed past the roller coaster and the vendors, sailing above the turnstiles and into the forest, her lips open in a silent scream.

"Claire, wake up. *Now!*" A boy's voice called out from far, far away. "I'm losing her, Clu, I'm going to drop her."

Suddenly Claire snapped back into her body with an enormous jolt. Her eyes popped open. "Where . . ." The word barely made it past her lips when she became aware of a horrible floating feeling, as if she were about to take a terrible fall. Her eyes focused on the ground, twenty feet below, and from the bottom of her lungs, she screamed.

"Give me your hand, Claire. Now!" A familiar voice shouted. Screaming, sobbing, Claire tried to lift her head. Somebody was holding on to her leg.

She struggled to right herself, but as hard as she tried she could barely get her arm to move. All the strength was gone from her limbs, and she felt light and limp as a leaf. "Help me!" she gasped through her tears.

"Claire, you can do this. You *have* to!" It was Jack's voice. His grip was so hard on her ankle it hurt, but his strength seemed to flow through him, right into her veins. Willing every muscle of her body to come alive, Claire managed to swing upward slightly and grab his hand.

"Hang on!" Jack ordered, as he met her eyes. He looked as scared as she felt. "Clu, I've got her."

Together they managed to scramble back on to the remains of the shattered platform of the tree house. They lay on their stomachs, gasping for air, Claire sobbing, Jack mumbling something to Clu about owing him one.

"How'd you know to come to the tree house?" Claire asked Fi shyly, a little while later. Jack and Clu had just helped her down from the tree, when Fi had turned up, pale and panicked. After catching their breath, they had headed back toward the

Avners'. Now they stood on the sidewalk, sheltered from view of the house by the front yard hedge.

"You told me yesterday. It was your old hideout. It took me a minute to add it all up," Fi explained, her hands still clammy after an hour. Her head was buzzing with "what ifs": What if Clu and Jack hadn't found the tree house? What if Claire hadn't gotten back to her body in time? What would have happened to Claire? Or Jack? Fi's stomach lurched. She forced a smile. "Anyway, it all worked out okay in the end."

"Thanks to you," Claire said, looking from Fi to Jack to Clu, then back to Fi again. She held up her hand for a high five. This time when Fi slapped it, there was a resounding *thwack* and the comfortable friendly feel of flesh to flesh.

"But now for the bad part," Claire said, gesturing to her house. Peering through the shrubbery, Fi could see Claire's parents. She put her finger to her lips and motioned for Claire to come and peek through the branches.

Mrs. Avner was pacing the front walk, a cell phone in her hand. She was punching in a number, at the same time she was speaking to her husband, who was checking his pager. "Don," she said to him, "I haven't really seen her since last night. How could this happen? The principal at the school said she left with the other kids at three o'clock. She always comes right home. I checked her room. She isn't there. I'm going to call the police."

"Man, you're really in trouble," Clu whispered, leaning over Claire's shoulder.

"But I'll deal with it," Claire said, catching Fi's eye.

"Whatcha going to tell them?" Jack asked.

Claire straightened up and made a face. "Nothing about astral projection, that's for sure. They'll think I've lost it big-time!" She grew thoughtful. "I'm just going to tell them the truth. That they're pushing me too hard, and I need some space—and time for fun." To Fi she said, "Wish me luck."

"You'll do okay," Fi said, then gave her a quick hug.

As Claire started for the driveway, her father's voice floated out toward the street. "I'm going to take the car and start looking for her. Keep the cell phone on."

"I'd better hurry," Claire said. She walked to the foot of the driveway, but before she headed for the house, she turned. "Thanks again. I guess I'm a little too big for that tree house."

Clu shifted from foot to foot. "Hey, no problem. I think Jack pretty much destroyed it anyway."

"With more than a little help from my friend here!" Jack pointed out a bit testily.

Claire put her hand on his arm. "Y'know, I'm expecting to see you guys next time you're in town. After all, you still owe me a stuffed animal."

Fi rolled her eyes, as Claire pecked first Clu, then Jack, on the cheek. Claire faced the driveway, caught sight of her parents, and sighed.

"Scared?" Fi asked.

"Yeah." Claire poked herself in the shoulder and gave a rueful laugh. "But I'm still here. I haven't gone off anywhere."

Straightening her back, and flipping her hair off her face, Claire marched down the driveway, shoulders squared. "Hey, Mom, Dad!" she called out.

"Claire," her mother gasped, as her father jumped out of the car. "Where have you been?" she cried, gathering Claire into her arms. "We've been worried sick about you."

"I know," Claire said. "And I think we've got to talk."

Fi watched a moment as they all headed into the house.

"I feel for her!" Clu muttered. "I *hate* those parent–child conferences!"

"Speaking of which." Fi squinted at the setting sun, then checked her watch. "We're going to have a major conference if we don't get back to the bus in the next fifteen minutes. It's time to hit the road again, and we are beyond late already."

Jack waited until they were out of earshot of the house. "She's a little crazy, but I like her."

"Hey, I don't care if she's a *ghost*. That is my future wife," Clu stated.

"Wife!" Fi stopped dead in her tracks. "I don't believe I'm hearing this," she muttered, quickening her pace.

Jack ignored her completely. To Clu he declared, "Well, that's gonna be a problem, considering she likes me better."

"She does not."

"She does."

Fi clapped her hands over her ears. "You guys. Get real here. You're fifteen going on sixteen— both of you. Tell me you're not talking marriage."

Ignoring Fi, Clu insisted to Jack, "She's just pretending to like you. That'll make things easier when we have you over for dinner so you can watch the kids."

Fi pressed her hands to her temples. *"Kids?* Did I hear the word 'kids'?"

Jack finally seemed to remember Fi actually existed. "Yeah, the love and marriage thing, little sister."

His voice was pure condescension.

But Fi didn't get mad. She had proof now. Their brains had astral projected—off into the stratosphere, or beyond.

"Did anyone ever tell you, you two are *so* beyond weird," Fi exclaimed, in a tone of utter disgust. "But I'm stuck with you anyway." Hooking her one arm through her brother's and her other through Clu's, she firmly steered them toward the bus and their next road stop.

so weird

Fi is a computer whiz with an obsession for all things weird.
Together with her brother, Jack, and their rock star mom, Molly,
they crisscross the United States while Mom jams with her band.
Along the way Fi tries to solve all kinds of supernatural mysteries—
everything from ghosts to UFOs—even the legend of Bigfoot.

From your
TV Room
to your
Library

So Weird: Escape
Available now

**So Weird:
Family Reunion**
Available now

So Weird: Shelter
Available now

So Weird: Strangeling
July 2000

APPEARING IN STORES
Spring 2000

SoWeird.com